The Clang Birds

By the same author . . .

QUICK AS DANDELIONS

RUBRICS FOR A REVOLUTION

PICNIC IN BABYLON: A PRIEST'S JOURNAL

ONE EYE AND A MEASURING ROD

NO PLACE FOR HIDING

TIGHT WHITE COLLAR

The Clang Birds

A NOVEL BY John L'Heureux

The Macmillan Company :: NEW YORK, NEW YORK

The Macmillan Company
866 Third Avenue, New York, N.Y. 10022
Collier-Macmillan Canada Ltd., Toronto, Ontario

Library of Congress Catalog Card Number: 72-77652
First Printing

Printed in the United States of America

for Elizabeth Bartelme

"The Clang Bird is a rare creature that flies in ever decreasing circles at ever increasing speeds until, with a terrible clang, it disappears up its own ass. It is only because of the will of God that the Clang Bird is not yet extinct."

St. Gommer, O.S.T.
Founder, Order of St. Thomas
Novissima Verba, 1717.

The Clang Birds

1

In the old house everyone was holy, or at least meant to be. They had intended it and they had taken vows. If what they said and what they did were not always the words and actions of holy men, that was because even holy flesh is weak and because intentions wander and because the vows had been made a long time ago. And so the seven Thomasite priests and twenty-three Thomasite Scholastics, whatever their true spiritual condition might have been, all lived in a state of official holiness in the old house on Winter Place.

In the new house, a crumbling duplex on Oak Road, protest would be the thing. Creative protest. Five of them would move in, forming an experimental religious community, a link between the lower-middle-class citizens among whom they would be living and the more exalted members of the University where all five attended classes. They had readied the new house for their arrival on September ninth. Since this was the seventh, however, and since it was almost midnight, they were in their rooms at the old house, living their ordinary Thomasite lives. All of them, that is, except George St. George and Reginald Body, both of them priests.

George was several streets distant, making love in his clumsy fashion to Natalie Meyer, a fellow graduate student much admired for the purity of her Middle English and the perfection of her breasts. They had met the previous spring and, in no time at all, had progressed from discussions of the Midlands dialect to oral recitations of the *Ancren Riwle* and so on to petting of a minor order. Natalie had spent the summer in New York with her mother who was on leave from the Kibbutz, and when she returned to Cambridge in late August, she and George had taken up where they left off.

He was slouched now on Natalie's daybed, running his fingers through strands of her long hair. It excited him terribly and to distract himself—he must not commit sin again, above all he must not—he reached for his glass of wine with his free hand. He had brought the wine himself, he reflected, and that perhaps was a mistake.

Natalie leaned more heavily against him and tucked her

tiny feet beneath her on the couch. This time, she was determined, she would be ready. Oh please, she thought, let it go all right, this once, just this once.

George put down the glass and let his hand slide from Natalie's delicate little shoulder to her back and down to her waist.

"So thin," he murmered.

"Mmmmm," she said.

"And tiny."

"Mmmmm."

His hand began to trace her ribs, stopping at the soft bulge of her breast. He could feel the skin, the nipple, beneath the thin stuff of her blouse.

"You're not wearing . . ."

"No."

He began to kiss her forehead, her eyelids, her upper lip, deliberately tantalizing her, refusing her tongue. He slid his hand beneath her blouse, shifting his long body as he did so, trying to stretch out beside her.

But his mouth was upon hers and his hand was hot and wet and their legs seemed tangled together. He reached down, fumbling, but before he could even unbuckle his trousers, his body shook violently, lunging against hers, and in a few seconds it was all over. He lay there, sticky and guilty, with all of the burden and none of the pleasures of sin.

"Oh God," he said, "what a shit I am."

"No, no," she said, "no."

"I am. That's what I am. I can't even sin properly."

"Don't worry," she said, gently rubbing the back of his neck. Natalie had had no experience with priests, but she had instincts and they served her well. "Don't worry. It's going to be all right."

"I'd better go home."

"You can stay and just talk for a while. I'd like that."

George stood and examined the dark stain on his trousers. "No, I have to be alone to savor my guilt."

He spoke only half ironically. He was aware that what he was savoring was not guilt but the realization that he had failed to achieve a set goal, something they would achieve together before very long.

On the following morning, George would confess his sins to Reginald Body who would tell him, as he had consistently told him, that he must break off his relationship with this girl. And George would resolve to do so. They would then, with the other Thomasite priests, concelebrate the noon Mass, Bob Moran playing his guitar and Sister Imelda smoldering with a holy passion, and that evening they would celebrate the Immaculate Conception at a feast preceded by three scotches, attended by champagne, and followed by Drambuie. Then, though he had intended just to write her a letter, George would stroll over to Natalie's apartment to explain that he must never see her again. And there on the daybed, slowed down by the quantity of alcohol and assisted by the patient, clever Natalie, he would for the first time perfectly achieve his set goal. He would spend the night with her improving his performance as the hours passed and the next morning he would return home guiltless.

But this evening when Natalie said to him,"You can stay and just talk for a while. I'd like that," George stood and examined the dark stain on his trousers, saying, "No, I have to be alone to savor my guilt."

And so he walked back to the old house on Winter Place where at one in the morning he met Reginald and the four Lollipops who had decided to walk him home.

Reginald had spent the evening at Dumfey's Cafe attending a secret meeting of priests and nuns and colorful laymen who had been derisively called lollipop revolutionaries by a Franciscan at the Business School. They were delighted at the slur, reminding themselves that Christians and Jesuits had come by their names in similar fashion, and so they called their group the Lollipop Conspiracy; this evening they had been plotting a raid on the local draft board.

"We've got to say Yes to life and No to everything that kills life." Bob Moran spoke with authority.

"Right. And that means fighting fire with fire," Sister Imelda said. "Even Christ tells us, 'I've come to bring fire upon the earth.' So I don't see why we have to exclude bombing from our plans. Or kidnapping. We could kidnap the local head of the draft board."

"No, no, no. You see that gets violent right away. Somebody *might* get hurt is the point. Or the guy we kidnap might have a heart attack. Some of those bastards, you never know.

"Well, look at Christ in the Temple," Sister Imelda said.

"We're off the point," Bob Moran said. "The big thing is to keep to the point. Now, we're all agreed that we'll knock off a draft board and napalm their cards. So the only thing is to decide when and then *act* on it." His right cheek quivered with the tick he was developing. This always happened whenever he spoke with authority, even though he knew he had the right to speak with authority, being a Jesuit and very nearly having been in on the Dow Chemical raid. Hoping to head off Sister Imelda, he looked at Reginald, "What do you think, Reg?"

Reginald returned his look. His eyes were wide and there was the trace of a smile around his mouth. He shrugged one shoulder deprecatingly. Bob Moran wondered now and then what Reginald was doing in the Lollipops in the first place.

Reginald sometimes wondered also. During the previous spring the University had experienced its celebrated Bust, when police were summoned to the newly liberated College Hall and, once there, charged at the unarmed students, cracking heads and collarbones with unnecessary enthusiasm. In the scramble Reginald, who was returning from a Newman Club meeting, paused to see what was happening and received for his curiosity a knee in the groin and, as he fell, a solid whack on the shin. From that moment he had been radicalized, he said, and at the invitation of Sister Imelda had begun to attend the Lollipops regularly. Unfortunately, he did not feel radicalized enough to contribute to the revolutionary talk anything except the charm of his presence, which they found considerable.

"Reg?" Bob Moran asked again, "what do you think?" He raised his hand to cover the flicker of skin on his cheek.

Reginald shrugged once more. "It's hard to say, Bob," and

he smiled. "It's the Spirit that moves."

All the others, priests and nuns and laymen, smiled at one another and nodded. Reg couldn't have been more right.

And so Reginald sat there, handsome and passive and a little miserable, waiting for the Spirit to move him to break down doors and burn draft cards. He glanced at his watch; he wished he were home like all the other Thomasites whose lives were good and simple and uncomplicated, except maybe George, and only God knew where George might be.

Reginald and the four Lollipops were standing in front of the house on Winter Place deep in a discussion of wire-tapping when someone approached them in the dark. They fell silent as the footsteps slowed and then stopped altogether. It was George.

"Oh, George," Reginald said, glad to drop the silly subject of wire-tapping.

"Good old George." Bob Moran, who disliked George, stuck out his hand. His cheek was still twitching.

"I spilled wine on my pants," George said, and they all stared at him in the dark. "I mean, I should go and wash it."

"I should go too," Reginald said a bit too eagerly.

"We all might as well go," Sister Imelda said, for without Reginald they had nothing but conspiracy to hold them together.

As the two men passed through the huge kitchen, George said ambiguously, "They can't seem to get enough of you, Reg."

"They do, though," Reginald said and he put off the

lights in the downstairs hall because now all the Thomasites were home.

All the Thomasites were home in the old house on Winter Place. A few of them were still studying, but most were in bed asleep. Billy Biggins was asleep and had been for an hour. Sean Kelly, who could never sleep, was in the bathroom gulping tranquilizers; he aspired to write poetry and felt that gave him license to depend at least upon the lesser drugs. Jim Doyle was at his desk studying a paper on skin grafts. And these were the five—Reginald, George, Billy, Sean, Jim—who were to move into the new house on Oak Road to begin a life of creative protest.

As it turned out, for reasons best known to himself and Natalie, George would not move into the new house at all. At the end of a month Superiors would select Hans Berger to replace him, much to everyone's chagrin. Hans would obey, not because of his devotion to obedience, though that was consummate, but because he saw in the command the finger of God pointing to the solution of his problem.

Hans' problem was of recent origin. As a boy in rural Minnesota he had led an exemplary life. He had said morning and evening prayers, served Mass, obeyed his parents. He had no great natural intelligence, but he substituted for this a stubbornness and a determination which allowed him to replace thinking with memory and which eventually got him a scholarship to a Thomasite high school. There he flowered; his memory was much praised and his purity of mind and body were silently and gratefully noted. Thus he graduated at the top of his class, convinced that whatever he wanted to accomplish required only the exercise of his inflexible will.

It was inevitable, then, that as if on a conveyor belt he left the high school and entered the novitiate, progressing grade by grade, course by course, until he emerged finally as an ordained priest, perfect as the will could make him. He was sent East to the University and there for a year continued his life of exemplariness.

But for the past three years he had been plagued by what he described to his confessor as "a sting of the flesh." What he meant was that once a month, as regular as the full moon, wildly and gleefully, he masturbated. He had prayed, he had sought counsel, he had read books. Nothing helped. Somewhere there had occurred a massive collapse of the will. And he was horrified when his confessor, a venerable old priest whose worst sin had been stealing wine from the sacristy, had told him to try to forget it, it probably wasn't a sin anyway. Hans thought back to his three years of depravity, those thirty-six damning acts, and set about finding a more strict confessor.

Now, on the eve of the Feast of the Immaculate Conception, Hans lay in bed saying the Rosary. His month was up and he had been hounded all through the day by sinful thoughts and desires, but he had followed his new confessor's advice and relaxed now, conscious of success. Twice that day he had stood beneath an icy shower and said over and over, "My Jesus, mercy, St. Joseph, defend me," and he had read St. Thomas à Kempis on the evils of the flesh. In bed now, still shivering from the freezing shower, he stretched and held all his muscles taut for a minute. He could feel the strength in his arms and legs, in the muscles of his stomach. He finished the Rosary and tucked it under his pillow. He stretched once more. He lay staring at the ceiling, trying to force his mind back to Kempis, back to Jesus and Joseph.

And then, as if it were not part of him, as if it had a life and will of its own, his sly hand crept beneath the sheets searching for the enemy.

A door closed. George had finally left off scrubbing his trousers. There was quiet throughout the house, some men still at their studies, some at prayer, most asleep. The house was voiceless, a house of prayer, of speechless meditation on the transitoriness of all things mortal. Silence everywhere. The only sound was the creak of springs and the frantic rustle of sheets as Hans Berger, wild and gleeful, flailed his pitiful organ.

That was in the old house, where everyone was holy or meant to be. In the new house, protest would be the thing. They would lead lives of radical Christianity, they would be poor and obedient and chaste, they would live in the world, in the crumbling duplex at 42 Oak Road. And they would start all this the day after the Feast. Nobody wanted to miss the Feast.

2

"A healthy apostle," St. Gommer often said, "is a witness for Christ, but a sick one is a burden to the community."

Thus feasts had been a large part of traditional Thomasite life ever since St. Gommer founded the order in France in the late 1600s. Gommer had been a man of great worldliness before his conversion; afterward, like St. Francis and St. Ignatius before him, he compensated for his early excesses of the flesh by austerities so severe that he permanently damaged his health. He feared similar fervor in his followers and so made a rule that on the greater holy days they should hold a feast, and he went on to specify varieties of fish and fowl and livestock that should be served. He specified even the order of their service, for he was meticulous in all the details of life.

"A sick apostle is kin to the Clang Bird," Gommer said, not bothering to explain.

In time, he died. Though in the course of the three centuries that followed his death, many sacred traditions passed away, though indeed even the vows themselves took on new and less taxing meanings, certain absolutes remained.

Feasts remained. Their service was less formal certainly, but the food was more lavish and the drink more rare. And so, though Thomasites often missed Mass and always missed Benediction, they never missed feasts. Feasts were a kind of permanence.

3

It was at the Midsummer Feast in July 1969 that a separate community was first proposed.

Summer had always been a bleak period for Thomasite feasts and over the years Father Sheehey, the Superior at Winter Place, had taken to celebrating St. Ignatius' day with only slightly less solemnity than he accorded St. Gommer himself. When some of the Fathers had objected to so much fuss over a Jesuit saint, Father Sheehey had reassured them that the celebration was secular rather than sacred, a toast to Brother Sun rather than to Father Ignatius, and he took care thereafter to refer to it as his Midsummer Feast.

Father Sheehey had invited outside guests, two Jesuits, a Franciscan, and a bewildered Monsignor, and they had all come early and eaten well. George, however, had arrived an hour late—he had met a summer student in the library stacks and had been telling her what he knew about Byron—and by that time the lobster salad was gone. So were the potato salad and the cold roast beef and the ham. George poured himself a scotch and drank it straight down. He poured himself another, larger this time, and then filled his plate with stuffed eggs and a stalk of celery since that was all that remained.

"Cleaned out," Bob Moran said, sounding to George even more Jesuitical than usual.

"Well, it's a Jesuit feast." George snapped at one of the eggs.

"You'll survive, Georgie. You've got that instinct." But George did not hear him, having already left the room.

Everywhere men were huddled in small groups. They were dressed according to the priestly fashion of the time in baggy trousers and wildly colored sport shirts, open at the throat. There was much laughter and loud talking as they drank the champagne which brought the meal to a close. George looked at them and instinctively knew what they were talking about: theology, sex, and sports, but especially sports. Fingering his tie, George said to nobody in particular, "So it was in the beginning, is now, and ever shall be, world without end. Amen." Nobody answered him. He finished his drink and went back for another, and just in time, since Father Sheehey was beginning to put away the scotch. Stingy bastard, George said to himself.

There was no one he cared to talk to, his life being lived for the most part outside the Thomasite community, and there were many he did not want to talk to. When he spotted Reginald miraculously alone, he joined him.

"Happy feast day," he said, trying to make it sound sarcastic.

"George. Good old George." Reginald had had a great deal to drink and stared hazily at George's plate. "Why are you eating all those eggs, George?"

"Because it just so happens there's nothing else to eat."

"You ought to have some lobster salad, George. It's delicious. Sean made it. Delicious, Sean."

Sean, whom George hated, joined them.

"Hi, Georgiepoo. How's your ass?"

George looked at him contemptuously and refused to answer.

"Sorry. I forgot you don't have things like that. George St. George, the assless wonder. Say, how come you're eating all those eggs?"

"I love eggs. I have a passion for eggs." George began to perspire.

"I hate eggs," Billy Biggins said through his nose. "I stuffed them. There were eighty-seven eggs and I stuffed them. But I wouldn't eat them. They're bad for you, George, if you have too many." He turned to Reginald. "Now *why* do you suppose anybody would want to eat only eggs?"

"Because he loves eggs; he has a passion for eggs," Sean said in a tight angry voice like George's.

George, uncertain whether he hated Sean's malice more than Billy's stupidity, exploded in a short but vitriolic denunciation of Father Sheehey, calling him a stingy bastard, a nosy old fart, and an eavesdropper. The explosion was received in silence since Father Sheehey was at this moment going from group to group filling brandy glasses, and George, hoping to appear less foolish, attacked instead the idea of living at Winter Place.

"Do you know what it costs?" he asked. "Do you realize each of us pays eight dollars a day for board and room here? Do you realize that's two hundred and forty dollars a month? That's one hell of a sum."

He paused to consider it himself. The stipend paid to Winter Place went directly from higher Superiors to Father Sheehey; since it did not pass through George's hands at all, he had never before thought of it as actual money.

"Think about that," he said.

They all thought about it; like George, they had never thought about it before.

"It's a scandal," George said. "I mean, just compare how the average graduate student lives to the way we live. *They* don't have any wall-to-wall carpeting, you can be sure of that. They don't have feasts on St. Ignatius' day. They don't . . ." but here his rhetoric got the better of him and he found himself saying, "What we ought to do is form a community of our own and really live the vows as they were intended. Radical Christianity."

To Sean and Billy this proposal was just more of George's rant; besides, they were still absorbing the two hundred and forty dollars. But to Reginald, recently radicalized and uncertain what to do about it, this sounded like inspiration. A community straight out of Acts of the Apostles sprang up before him. Everyone would share decisions. And share the work. They could have prayer sessions together. Mass at the kitchen table.

"George," he said, "you're a fucking genius."

All that evening and late into the night, first over a bottle of Cutty Sark that belonged to Sean and then over bourbon stolen from Father Sheehey's liquor closet (George had the key), Reginald and George and Sean and Billy discussed the new community, a protest community, growing warm in their feelings for each other as they talked. By two in the morning the decision had been made. They would write their higher Superiors and inform them of their plans for a new community. Inform, not request; no sense starting badly. They would begin at once to look for a large apartment or a small house. They would pool their scholarship money and the support money paid by their several Superiors to the Superior of Winter Place. They would be independent and poor and live lives of radical Christianity.

After they had slept and wakened, of course, the previous night's discussion seemed altogether unreal. But Reginald remained enthusiastic and Billy Biggins—though he kept asking "*Why* would we want to do this?"—was made enthusiastic by the possibilities of house-hunting: interviews, the juggling for price, the endless details to be checked over and over again. Sean was appalled at the thought of living with George and George himself had already begun to hint at difficulties with his thesis, difficulties he hoped might later extricate him from the awful plan. But since he had begun it, he went along with it, at least officially.

When they made their request to higher Superiors—they had wisely decided to begin their lives of protest only after moving into the new house—permission was granted at once, not, as they thought, because they had so persuasively argued their case for radical Christianity, but because their rooms at Winter Place were needed for a rather larger incoming class. Superiors insisted on only one point: that there be no less than two priests and no more than three scholastics living in the house. It took them no time at all to select Jim Doyle, a medical student of formidable intellect, who was always pleasant, always interesting, and whom nobody really knew.

Jim had entered from medical school only three years earlier and had been swept through the course of studies by Superiors who were anxious lest he get bored and go away. As a consequence, he had experienced none of the traditional Thomasite training and found himself—the same quiet, dedicated, professional man he had been, only now with the vows of a Thomasite—back at University medical school working for his M.D. He looked at George, Billy, Sean, and Reginald, foresaw clearly what the year with them would be and, swallowing twice, agreed to join them.

In this way, at a Thomasite feast, the protest community on Oak Road came into being, in large part because George was stuck with the stuffed eggs and took out his wrath on Father Sheehey. That patient old man took the news of the new house with the equanimity with which he greeted all things.

He was over seventy. He had taught philosophy in his earliest years and after that had been Chaplain, in rapid succession, to an insane asylum, the United States Army, the Sisters of Notre Dame. For the thirty years that followed he had been a Superior, inured to the whims and peculiarities of his subjects, amused to observe how few the forms of madness actually were. He prayed and he worked and, whenever the liturgical calendar allowed, he gave a feast.

He wished them well at 42 Oak Road; he nodded and smiled and poured the brandy.

4

"Mucky and Fucky McReedy got stomped in the subway."

The word ran up and down Oak Road even before the ambulance reached the hospital.

"Mucky and Fucky got stomped by niggers."

Michael, age eleven, was called Mucky because his name was Michael. Francis, age twelve, was called Fucky because of his sexual precocity. And to their Irish gang, there was something agreeable about the sound of Mucky and Fucky McReedy.

Anyway, they were stomped in the Park Street subway at rush hour one evening in the middle of summer.

They had been to Fenway Park to see the Red Sox play Detroit. Detroit won and Michael groaned, not because he cared about the Sox, but because he had made a dollar bet and lost. Angry and looking for trouble, he deliberately peed on his brother's foot when they went to the Men's Room.

"You did that on purpose."

"Didn't."

"You want to get hurt?"

"I didn't do it on purpose, Fucky. Swear to God."

Francis wasn't sure Michael had done it on purpose, but he punched him in the face just in case.

The subway train was jammed with people coming home from the game. Fathers sweated from the beer and the heat and their bored twitching children. Mothers shifted from leg to leg, eager to get home to their kitchens where they could lose their patience in peace. Around everyone's knees and waists children stood, pushing, poking one another with balloon sticks and pennants. Michael landed one of the little girls a quick kick and she stopped her carrying on.

Two blacks stood on the other side of the car, bumping one another with their hips. Michael spotted them, and since they were younger and smaller than he, he curled his lower lip down until it touched his chin, rolling his eyes toward heaven. Finally, just as his eyes began to hurt, one of the blacks saw him and nudged the other one to look.

Across the fidgeting children and the suffering parents, the four boys stared at each other. And then, as if on cue, Michael and Francis tipped their heads far back and chanted to the ceiling, "Neeeeeee-gro." They checked to see what effect they were having, but the two blacks were merely standing there, staring, no emotion whatsoever on their faces.

"Neeeee-gro," Michael chanted again and again until a man standing near him decided to intervene.

"Little boy," he said, "stop that. Stop that right now."

"Neeeee-gro," Michael went on.

"Did you hear what I said. I said stop that!"

"Fuck off," Michael said. "Neeee-gro."

The train pulled into Park Street and the McReedys wriggled through the crowd and out the door, careful to give the two blacks a good shove. Then they ran, laughing maniacally, down the stairs for the connecting train to Cambridge.

A drunk was propped against one of the huge cement pillars and the McReedys were whispering together about how to get his wallet, if he had a wallet, when the two young blacks charged down the stairs with two larger blacks behind them. The McReedys, old hands at disappearing, slipped behind the pillar and moved little by little down the entire length of the station until there was nowhere else to go. They huddled together behind the last pillar, and that was where the blacks found them.

"Hey, man. You wanted some trouble, man?" and the four closed in.

"It was a joke, that's all."

"You wanted some trouble, man. We're here. You got trouble now, man. You got plenty trouble." His voice was very quiet.

The two men began to push Michael and Francis back and forth between them.

"Here, man, you take him. I don't want him." He shoved Francis at his friend.

"He a white man. He too good for me, man. You better keep him." And he shoved Francis back.

The shoves grew more violent as Francis and Michael jerked and tumbled back and forth. Michael was terrified and, being upright for a moment, tried to make his escape by a quick dodge to the right. One of the blacks caught him by the belt and tugged hard. Michael fell flat and, seeing the black faces bending over him, immediately got hysterical.

"Fucky, Fucky," he shouted for help.

The blacks had intended only to rough him up a bit but now they were furious.

"Call me fucky, man, you get it." And he laid a solid punch on Michael's jaw.

"Fucky," Michael shouted. And the more he shouted, the more they punched, until his face was bloody from a cut over the eye and his lip was split where they knocked the tooth out. Francis lay beside him unconscious, with a broken leg.

An ambulance took them to Boston City Hospital where, that afternoon, Mrs. McReedy relieved the dullness of her life with an orgy of combined grief and vituperation. Early in the evening Officer McReedy picked them all up in the cruiser and, with the siren wailing, drove them home to the crumbling duplex at 42 Oak Road.

5

PROTEST!

Poverty—?

Chastity—?

Obedience—?

The rest of the paper was alive with little sketches of

eyes: closed eyes, staring eyes, tilted eyes, Oriental eyes, Sophia Loren's eyes.

Reginald had given up trying to make out a list of topics for discussion. He had gotten only as far as obedience when it occurred to him that everything that could be said on these things had been said already, or at any rate he had heard all he cared to hear. And yet, if they were to be a protest community, they had to have something fairly basic to protest about.

He stopped doodling and wrote on a new sheet of paper:

PROTEST!

Poverty–not having things.

Chastity–not having people.

Obedience–not having . . .

He had been about to write "not having free will," but that was scarcely an ideal for a protest community. Well, that could be one of the points for discussion; what the hell was obedience supposed to mean? He whimpered quietly, a strange puppy noise, high and pleading, a habit he was acquiring.

Sean appeared suddenly in the doorway. He folded his hands before his heart in the manner of a concert singer and recited:

"Ladybug, ladybug,
Fly away home.
Your house is on fire,
Your children are all fucked up."

"I made up the last part myself," he said and disappeared up the stairs.

Protest community, nothing; it was a madhouse. Reginald returned to his list. Poverty . . . he went through all of it again. What *were* they protesting anyway? "The religious life" flashed through his mind, but he blinked and let it pass. Crazy thoughts kept coming to him these days. He whimpered again.

They must have a discussion; that was final. But discussions didn't really work. So far, they had failed to produce any concrete results, not even a common resolution on what a protest community was all about. He began to perspire.

"What are we all about?" he said aloud and slammed his pencil on the desk. He looked around, foolish.

Reginald was alone in his room in the new house on Oak Road where they had lived for two weeks. What with the Lollipops, the smoldering Sister Imelda, and now a crumbling duplex slung around his neck, Reginald was beginning to show the strain. They had not been an easy two weeks; the first one, though, had been the hardest.

Despite what had seemed elaborate preparation, nothing was ready when they arrived on the morning of September ninth. All the scrubbing and sweeping and tossing out of junk appeared to have been done at some other house; certainly this one was filled with dirt and dust and old furniture. There were an exceptional number of maimed tables: three-legged tables, coffee tables, and something that appeared to be a writing table, with its sloping surface and profusion of ink stains. Mattresses covered the living room floor and in the front bedroom five iron bed frames, as yet unassembled, were propped between an overstuffed sofa and a wicker porch chair. A rolled carpet slouched drunkenly in a corner. All the furniture had been scrounged from the attics and cellars of relatives. All of it was junk.

Reginald and Sean stood at the door, numb.

Billy was doing the grocery shopping. Jim was at the hospital, George was in bed recovering from his athletic evening with Natalie. It was up to them.

"I'm going to throw up," Sean said. He lay down on one of the mattresses.

Sun was pouring in the open door and, for one moment, Reginald thought of turning his back on the room, closing the door, and walking away forever. Only for a moment. And then, as he had always done, he began slowly and logically to do one thing at a time. He dragged a mattress upstairs and after it, piece by piece, a bedstead. In half an hour he had assembled a bed.

Sean was amazed. He had lain on his back watching Reginald come and go, listening to the thuds upstairs as Reginald banged and wrenched the iron slats into their grooves. It would all go away, he was sure, if only he waited long enough. Finally, out of curiosity, he went upstairs and there, amazingly, was a bed. He knew that from the chaos downstairs a completed bed could be extracted, but he knew it only as an idea. To see it done, to see an actual bed emerge from the jumbled piles of iron and ticking, struck him as something miraculous. He began to help. Another bed emerged and then another. This is how poems get made, he was thinking, a little bit of chaos is wrestled into submission. The more he thought, the more excited he grew and the harder he worked. Reginald began to wonder what was wrong, Sean was so strangely silent.

When Billy returned from Economart, the beds and mattresses had been cleared from downstairs and all the tables had been piled in the kitchen. Sean was vacuuming the rug, a threadbare imitation Persian, and Reginald was standing watching him.

"You haven't done much," Billy said, adding, as they both rounded on him, "but of course there's only been the two of you." In the continued silence, he took in their sweaty clothes and angry faces and added, his voice shooting up an octave, "Now *why* would I say a thing like that?"

There were other minor irritations:

The groceries would not be delivered until the following day.

The refrigerator would not be delivered until the following week.

There were no shower curtains and the bathroom was flooded.

One of the boys next door kept up an incessant drumming with his plaster cast.

George had come over—the phone was not working—to say he would not be moving in for a few days.

Suddenly they all seemed to hate one another.

The rest of the week was much the same. Billy had followed Father Sheehey's advice and had bought groceries in bulk. The food, when it arrived a day late, was enough to supply them for weeks, and within hours, everyone on Oak Road knew that the Thomasites ate like kings.

In time the refrigerator came and they filled it with the chops and steaks they had been storing in a plastic trash-can filled with ice. The plumber came. The telephone repairman came. Life in a protest community began to look possible.

Francis McReedy sat on the front porch all week banging his plaster cast against the steps. He overheard everything that was said and done in the house and he reported it, with a coloring of his own, to his interested mother and to anyone else who would listen. By the end of the week protest had taken on new meanings for everyone on Oak Road.

Routine of a sort took over during the second week. Everyone cleaned his own room. Sean cooked. Billy and Jim did dishes. Reginald looked after the kitchen, living room, bathroom. The system, they discovered, worked surprisingly well. In the morning, each made his own breakfast and left for the University. They saw one another in the evening when they made drinks and pottered about the kitchen getting in Sean's way as he prepared dinner. And then they went off on their separate ways to study or to plot or to wear out the evening complaining about the sterility and irrelevance of their courses.

By the second week life in the protest community was the same as life at Winter Place, except more bothersome, since they now did their own cleaning and cooking and had no one to blame that things were not better. By the end of that week Reginald had begun to wonder why they had put themselves to so much trouble, merely to achieve discomfort.

"Discomfort is not virtue," he said aloud. He looked around and was embarrassed to find Jim at the door looking back at him.

"You cracking?" Jim said. He shifted his medical books from one arm to the other. "Better get a doctor."

"Hi. No, I'm trying to make a list of . . ."

"It's Doctor Jimmy in his little white suit," Sean said, halfway down the stairs. "How they hanging, Doctor?"

Jim only shook his head. Reginald tilted his chair back, his knees propped against the desk. Sean's arrival was the end of anything serious.

"Listen to this, Doc:

> 'Ladybug, ladybug
> Fly away home,
> Your house is on fire . . .' "

Jim interrupted him. "Your children have V.D."

"No, but that's very good. Very good. Shows you're becoming a true Thomasite." And then in a perfect imitation of Billy Biggins, Sean sang through his nose, "Now *why* would anyone want to do that."

The kitchen door slammed and Billy came in whistling. He had done well in the first quiz on "Measuring Personality Traits" and he was in high spirits.

"You're probably wondering why I've called you all together this afternoon," he said, and was astounded when they burst into wild laughter.

For years his contemporaries had been in silent agreement about Billy's stupidity. Since no one ever knew quite how to begin a conversation with him, everyone always waited for him to speak first. And so now his tired comment, coming unexpectedly, seemed to them improbably funny. They laughed some more.

Thus was born Billy's later reputation for wit. For the rest of his life he would always say the obvious, and on those rare occasions when he said something unexpected, even if it were not very funny, Thomasites would look at one another wide-eyed, pleased: Billy Biggins was a wit after all. In time, Billy would come to believe it himself.

But now they all stood at Reginald's door, laughing excessively, accomplices in the discovery of Billy's wit.

The good weather accounted in part for their new feeling, and of course being settled into the new house was a help, but the principal fact remained: they were all good men, each in his way, and they were . . . well . . . good.

Such was their feeling and Sean put it into words.

"Hey, let's all have a beer," he said, "together."

And they did, except for Sean himself who hated beer and had a Tom Collins instead. Billy for the first time seemed endurable and Jim was sitting there, drinking instead of passing through on his way to the laboratory or the hospital or his midnight studies. And good old Reg. No, they weren't a bad group at all.

A discovery like this deserved a celebration.

"Why don't we have a party?" Sean said. "We ought to do something about having that party."

"What party?"

"For Oak Road. For the little people of Cambridge."

And so they had a discussion after all, not about radical Christianity as Reginald had planned, but about the practical aspects of holding open house for the neighbors: to get to know them, to let them see that Thomasites were ordinary human beings, to open the Irish ghetto to an awareness of the blacks, the war, the underprivileged. They talked like this when they drank.

The telephone rang. George St. George would not be moving in with them after all. His reasons, he said, were spiritual ones and he was not free to discuss them. Everyone was annoyed at first, but after a moment it didn't seem to matter. Who needed George anyway? Sean was openly relieved.

The party was the thing, the open house. They would just talk and get to know the neighbors—the McReedys Senior appeared to avoid them for some reason; not a good beginning. Maybe some of the younger people would want to sing. Jim could play his guitar. And there would be cookies and coffee. And beer, but nothing harder. They would invite everyone on the street. Radical Christianity seemed once more a possibility. They set the date for October tenth, a Friday.

On Tuesday of that week they pushed invitations through the letter slots up and down Oak Road. On Wednesday and Thursday they cleaned the house and worried. On Friday Sean baked dozens of cookies: chocolate, butter, spice. They argued all during dinner whether or not Sean should cut his hair, which was now reaching shoulder length. It was finally agreed that in the interest of authenticity he should be allowed to keep it.

That evening, scrubbed and combed and dressed in their baggy trousers and sports shirts, they waited for their guests. An hour went by and they began to feel nervous and, in some unspecified way, foolish. What if no one came? They were all thinking it but no one said it. The kitchen clock ticked and ticked while they sat in silence, waiting.

While the Thomasites on Oak Road sat waiting for guests who might never come, Hans Berger was keeping a vigil of a different sort. On waking that morning he had congratulated himself that at last he had made it through a month without his sting of the flesh. Almost at once, as if God were punishing him for his presumption, he felt himself stiffen magnificently. He fled to the shower where, his teeth chattering in the icy water, he sang the Ave Maria three times through.

Now, in early evening, Hans returned once more from the shower, dressed, and fell to his knees. "My Jesus, mercy," he said, "St. Joseph, defend me," and he buried his face in his hands. Automatically he rattled off an Our Father and a Hail Mary, but even as he prayed, one hand crept from his face to the bed and finally fell limp to the floor. As he launched into the Glory Be to the Father, the hand grasped his knee and began to work its way, slowly, up his leg. Clearly, prayer alone was not going to work.

Vigorous exercise, that was what. He leaped to his feet. "We are men of the will," he said, bending over to touch his toes. Though he took some pride in his physical condition, he was seriously overweight, and he grunted as his hands stopped several inches short of the floor. Valiantly he tried again. And again. "We are men of the will, we are men of the will." He gave up after five attempts.

One of the secrets of Hans' intellectual success in the Thomasites was his memory book. All through the years of study, while others spent their free time writing poems or reading novels or chopping wood, Hans sat with a book and a notebook, copying passages from one into the other. These were carefully selected "thoughts," as he called them, and he would commit them to memory and later to appropriate exam papers and sometimes, startling everyone, he would spout one off in conversation.

Desperate now, he turned to his memory book. "A man who exposes himself to only one point of view can never be a historian—he is merely the member of a fashionable political cult." Wonderful. He repeated this slowly four times, but his mind wandered and very soon he found himself wringing his hands and pacing.

He knelt down. "Dear God," he prayed, "give me some sign that despite this sting of the flesh, I will not be damned. I will accept whatever sufferings You send if only You will let me know I will not be damned." And then as an afterthought he added, "Purest heart of Mary, I put my trust in thee."

At that moment the phone rang and in another moment

They stored their meat in a trash can full of ice, or at least they used to.

They drank night and day.

Sean cooked highbrow dishes and was probably—this was not said openly—a "morphodite." Anyhow he was certainly a hippy, with all that hair.

The doctor took care of niggers and spics without charging, which was discrimination. Besides, how could a priest be a doctor; it was a sin.

They had no chapel for saying Mass and there was no evidence that they did any religious things at all. Michael and Francis had kept watch and knew.

Sean wore jockey shorts and the others wore boxers.

The FBI or the CIA had tapped their phone.

The conclusion was obvious: they were a bunch of Communists. No one on Oak Road went to the Thomasite open house.

The four Thomasites, unaware of their Communism, settled back with their drinks, annoyed, disappointed, and a little relieved. It probably had not been such a good idea anyway. Later, perhaps, when they'd been in the neighborhood for some time and people had gotten used to them, perhaps then they . . .

"Who gives a shit anyhow," Sean said and no one contradicted him.

They talked and they drank, consoling themselves in their annoyance and embarrassment. It was dark outside and quiet, even the motorcycle noises were barely audible in the distance. They talked and they drank and time passed.

By midnight a snug feeling had crept into the room, as if they had once again discovered Billy's wit.

Reginald lapsed into one of his silences. He looked at Billy, whose tiny eyes darted from speaker to speaker, his face pinched in a double effort to keep his voice under control and to think of something to say. He looked at Jim; what was it about Jim? He was generous and patient and evidently holy, but there was something else, a solitariness about him. And Sean. Sean performed–chattering, imitating, improvising bawdy limericks–and then hated himself for performing, fell silent, drank some more, and performed all over again. That's how they are, Reginald thought, making no judgment, and went to the kitchen for another bag of Fritos.

They drank. They talked. They were as close to one another as they ever would be.

Reginald was happy and he hummed while he washed the glasses and emptied the ashtrays and cleared the kitchen table for tomorrow's breakfast. In his room, he shuffled through the little mountain of notes and memos that littered his desk until he found the paper headed PROTEST! He read it through and smiled. What did it matter anyhow. The paper slipped from his hand, made a little arc, and landed in the wastebasket.

"And that about takes care of protest," he said, and tumbled into bed.

For some reason he could not sleep. He tossed from one side to the other. He lay on his back. He tried consciously relaxing from his feet up. Finally he began to doze, but then just as he was drifting into sleep, he saw a picture of the four Thomasites talking and drinking while the minutes and then the hours ticked by.

"Oh, fuck them all," he said aloud and woke himself up. Reginald did not sleep at all that night.

6

"Why can't we just talk?" Natalie said.

"Come on to bed," he said.

"Honestly, George, ever since that time . . . we never talk any more. All we do is go to bed."

"Come on to bed," he said, nuzzling her.

"What about Middle English?" she said.

"Screw Middle English," he said.

"Oh, George."

Resigned, she began to tug off her sweater.

"Come on to bed," George said, naked already.

7

"Talk is the opiate of the people," Sister Imelda said. "Here it is the last day of September and still we haven't done anything."

The Christian Brothers nodded. Reginald examined his shoe. Sister Gunnekild chewed on her lip.

"Right, sure," Bob Moran said, "but what? Once you rule out draft boards, there's damned little left."

As a Jesuit, he felt he ought to be doing what his fellow Jesuits were doing, but the Lollipops had been unable to agree on what draft board they should liberate or how the liberation should be conducted. In a moment of hurt pride Bob had proposed shelving the whole idea until after the Spock trial. Incredibly, the motion had been seconded and passed before he could take back his hasty words. The Lollipops subsequently had found themselves short of causes.

"The thing is," Sister Imelda said, "that we're either pagans or Christians. And I say if we're pagans, then we ought to act like pagans, because nothing matters. But if we're Christians, then we ought to act like Christians. I mean, look at Bonhoeffer."

"Who's Bonhoeffer?" one of the Christian Brothers asked.

Sister Imelda looked at him in disbelief. "What I'm getting at," she said, "is that we've got a moral obligation to do something about the war and the poor and the Chicanos. For instance, look at all the grapes on sale in the Square. I think we ought to protest that. I mean, we could boycott, we should get everybody to boycott. Hey, what we ought to do is just throw everything into the street, like Christ cleansing the Temple."

The Christian Brothers nodded. Reginald looked up from his shoe and then looked back. Sister Gunnekild started to say something but turned to Bob Moran instead.

"Oh God," he said, "If it isn't bombing or kidnapping, it's stomping grapes."

"Well, we *should*," Sister Imelda said. "We've got to do *some*thing."

In the silence that followed, the clock struck midnight and September became October while the Lollipops sat and did nothing. At the other end of the campus, however, something was happening which would provide the Lollipops with their first opportunity for protest.

A house was burning down. It was an old rambling two-story house used as office space for teaching assistants in economics. No one was in it, and as it contained nothing of value except the unfinished dissertations of four teaching assistants, the people gathered for the fire were in generally high spirits.

No spirits were higher than those of the Board of Overseers. The house had been ancient and ugly, a small area of blight on the most valuable piece of property owned by the University. The house was something of a landmark, however, and the Overseers feared even to suggest pulling it down; some damned fool would surely sue to have the place declared a historic building and that would mean a counter-suit, years of delay, and a cool million in payoffs. The fire was an unmixed blessing, they thought, and the next morning newspapers carried photographs of the building in flames and, lower on the page, a small notice saying that the University would level what remained of the building and erect in its place a ten-story drama center. Everyone approved, or almost everyone, and the Overseers relaxed and congratulated one another.

The Overseers had not counted on the ingenuity of protest groups, however, and on the following day there were angry editorials in the underground sheets and even in the campus paper. People in Somerville were burning, the papers said, while the University fiddled. Families on relief were living in rat-infested tenements while the University staged absurdist drama in a ten-story superdome. Down with dead drama! Up with living people! Off the University! They ended with demands for a ten-story apartment building which would house none but minority groups.

The Overseers wept. History nuts were one thing but, as they had all recently learned, there was no fighting minority groups. Instant retreat was called for. At once they announced that the drama center had been only one of several proposals; that a number of community-oriented uses for the property were under consideration: a health center, for instance, with a gigantic swimming pool for Puerto Ricans.

But already it was too late. That afternoon placards appeared all over the campus announcing a giant protest rally for the morning of October the third.

The Lollipops agreed to meet before the rally and march as a group. At ten in front of College Hall, Bob Moran had said, and now here it was already ten and Sister Imelda was nowhere in sight. She had insisted on picking up Reginald at the duplex on Oak Road and walking with him to College Hall.

They must all be there by now, Reginald thought, and

looked out the front window for the seventh time. No Imelda. "Christ, women make me sick," he said aloud. He tugged at his roman collar which was plastic and made his neck sweat. "Clerics," he said, "God!" He began to wonder what she might wear, for it was understood that, whatever their ordinary garb might be, priests and nuns always wore clerical dress for protest marches. Almost at once she appeared and, although she was wearing the habit abandoned by her order only the year before, Reginald was unprepared for the sight of it. Usually she wore a dark-blue dress that stopped at her knees and, to indicate she was a nun, a sort of veil, a tiny square of cloth that attached to the crown of her head and hung to her shoulders. But today she was wearing the old habit, a full black gown with a starched white bib. It was peculiarly feminine and becoming, he thought, but then he saw that with it she wore not the old waist-length veil but the new one, a wisp of a thing perched incongruously on top of her head. He blushed and moved away from the window. "Ain't nobody here but us freaks," he said, and went outside to join her.

"Wow!" she said, beaming. "Hi!"

"Hi. We're going to be late."

"It's the sign," she said, instantly penitent. "I had a lot of trouble carrying it."

The sign, a large square of cardboard stapled to a carrying stick, proclaimed in red letters "The play's *not* the thing! People are!"

"What do you think? No good?"

"No. It's all right. It's to the point."

"Oh, gosh, thanks. Do you think so? Wow! I mean, really, thanks. I made it myself." She thought for a wild moment of hugging him, but only as a friend, a brother even, he was so nice, but then he was saying, "Come on, let's move it," and that brought her back to reality.

Reginald could see what she meant about carrying the sign. There was no way to hold it but straight up. Picketing with a crowd was one thing, but carrying a sign through the streets and across the campus all by yourself was quite another. Especially in monkey suits.

"Oh God," he said.

"You see? Try it over your right shoulder. That's how I did it."

The walk to the campus was an agony. An old woman followed them for a block shouting, "Communists, go back to Russia," and a grocery store owner stood at his shop door tossing pennies at them as they passed. Two squad cars stopped them to ask where they were picketing; the second was driven by Officer McReedy who made a show of staring straight ahead. "Commies," he said as he drove away, "traitors to God and country." And then they had the ill luck to pass the playground of the Cambridge grammar school at recess time. A hundred small children lined the wire fence shrieking and pointing. "Look at the hippies," they shouted, "Hippies, go home," and, "Go take a bath, you stink." Reginald walked firmly ahead, his eyes fixed on the pavement, Sister Imelda at his side, while he told himself over and over that never again would he wear clerics to a rally. At last they reached the University grounds.

Here, picket signs were no more unusual than trees and no one stared at foreign or fantastic clothing. They knew they were home. Sister Imelda, feeling not unlike Joan of Arc, insisted that Reginald surrender the sign.

"Well, there you are!"

"Bob! And Gunnie! Oh, how groovie!"

Bob Moran and Sister Gunnekild were with a small group of picketers in clerical dress. Sister Imelda darted from one to the other, wriggling with delight, telling them of the indignities she and Reginald had suffered on their way to the rally. Everyone was horrified and pleased.

"I love your sign," one of the Christian Brothers said to her, obviously unhappy with the one Bob Moran had brought. That sign said "Freedom NOW!" which, while not especially appropriate, was the only one Bob had had at hand that morning and, besides, he had pointed out, freedom is never irrelevant.

"You're a dear," she said and, unable to think of his name, made up for it by joining him in the picket line.

The burned building stood, gutted and lopsided, on a large corner lot bordered on three sides by streets. Next to the building stood a crane, gleaming yellow, with a fifty-foot arm from which hung a wrecking ball. University Overseers, who had rushed in the first wrecking apparatus they could come by, had wisely decided to suspend all operations until threats of disruption had passed, and so there was no one working the crane; there were no signs of workmen anywhere.

Still, it promised to be a successful day. Two of the three

streets had been blocked off by police to give the protesters more room to mill about and to give the squad cars easier access to any potential trouble spot, though there seemed no likelihood of trouble. The scene, in fact, was relaxed, almost festive. A man dressed in the stars and stripes of Uncle Sam was selling balloons. The operators of two ice-cream vans were quarreling furiously about whose territory was being violated while a third did a brisk business in ice cream. There were mothers pushing babies in strollers and there were dogs darting everywhere through the crowd. It was like a hundred such rallies, half picnic, half desperation.

Picketers strolled the sidewalks on the three sides of the lot and then circled back; the fourth side had been the back yard of the building and, littered as it was with trash cans and window panes and broken shingles, nobody wanted to walk there. Besides, the snaking circular motion of the double line gave the picketers a chance to talk to their friends, some of whom they never saw except socially at protest meetings. The weather, moreover, was perfect for picketing, warm, with a light western breeze.

For the next two hours they continued their revolutions. Eventually some drifted off to get lunch, others to change shoes; picketing was a tiring business. The midday heat was beginning to thin ranks even further and, since they were not obstructing work, many began to wonder if it wasn't time to proclaim a victory and go home. Some of the more radical elements formed small knots of three and four to discuss what ought to be done. Obviously something had to happen to keep up people's interest. Chanting was out; nobody chanted any more unless there was somebody around to infuriate. Baiting the police wasn't a good idea; that was best reserved for purely political conflicts, preferably racial in nature. Destroying the crane would be a perfect symbolic protest against both University and big business, but with so many police around, there would be no possibility of doing the crane any real harm before they were busted. And so they whispered in small huddles while the police, stationed every five feet around the four sides of the lot, shifted from leg to leg and watched them intently, fingering all the while the handles of their revolvers.

The balloon man was the one who finally did something.

"Outasight!" he said to Sister Imelda, pointing to her sign. "A gas!"

"Oh, it's you," she said, "Hi!" She recognized him as a fellow student in her course on Creative Christianity, a tall emaciated boy who had no friends. "I'm glad you like it; I made it myself."

"Hey, listen. I got it," he said. "This is gonna be great. Here, hold these. Gimme that." And he handed his balloons and his money belt to the Christian Brother. He took Sister Imelda's sign and with one punch tore it from its holder. Then with a key he bored two holes in the sign, attached a balloon string to either end as if he were going to hang it from a wall, but instead put the loop over his head so that the sign hung down his back.

"Voilà," he said, turning his back to them and posing. "Now listen," he said to the Christian Brother, "I want you to release a balloon about every thirty seconds. Got that? Like this." And he released a balloon. A few people turned to watch it drift skyward. He released another. "Hey," somebody shouted, "look at the balloons." He drifted away from the Christian Brother, calling backwards to him, "One every thirty seconds."

Another balloon rose and then another. Everyone had stopped marching now and had turned to watch. Even the police were fascinated.

It took only another minute for the balloon man to step between two policemen and sprint across the lot to the crane. He had scrambled into the cab and from the cab up onto the arm before anyone noticed him. Three policemen ran at him from their places in the line, the others shifting to cover the empty spaces, hands once again nervously at their revolvers.

But the situation was hopeless. The three policemen shouted at him and he waved back. They ordered him down and he gave them the victory sign. One of them screamed that he was under arrest and the crowd burst into cheers. Meanwhile, agile as an acrobat, he kept climbing up the long thin arm. The policemen fell silent; it was out of their hands now.

From his patrol car Officer McReedy called for a fire engine. They would probably have to take him off the crane with a fire ladder. Think of the money wasted, think of the taxpayers.

The crowd around the lot watched the figure in stars

and stripes scramble up the boom, using the steel struts as casually as if they were stairs. Halfway to the top he struck a pose and waved. Everyone cheered.

"But what's he going to do?"

"He's got a sign."

"Maybe he's going to jump. You know, the symbolic death of America."

"No shit. Beautiful!"

Speculation was wild and yet, by the time he was near the top, it was clear to everyone that he was going to hang the sign around the wrecking ball.

Someone began to clap rhythmically. Someone else began to sing "When the Saints come marching in," and it was picked up by the Lollipops, and almost at once the entire crowd was swaying from side to side, clapping and singing.

The balloon man reached the top of the arm and waved: Uncle Sam on a wrecking ball. The crowd stopped singing and burst into a prolonged cheer. At last something had happened.

He hugged the steel struts with his legs and began to ease the sign around to the side and lift it over his head. But as he did so, he lost his footing, and suddenly, horribly, his legs swung away from the towering steel crane and he hung there by one hand, his feet kicking at the empty air.

The crowd gasped and went silent. And then his leg struck one of the steel struts, he hooked his foot around it, and then his other foot, and he was safe. The crowd breathed again.

This time he slipped the loop deftly over his head. He

climbed a bit higher so that the end of the steel arm thrust into his belly. Supported in this way, he had his two hands free. He leaned down and tied a kind of noose around the cable attached to the ball. The sign slid a foot and caught. A slight breeze moved the sign from side to side, "The play's *not* the thing! People are!"

Everyone shouted and clapped their hands. Sister Imelda was jumping up and down. The police smiled in spite of themselves.

Fifty feet in the air, the balloon man waved and grinned and gave the peace sign. And then, with no warning, one of his feet came away from the struts, and while they watched in disbelief, the stripes and the stars rippled and blurred as the balloon man, with a small scream a hurt puppy might make, cartwheeled into the air and plummeted to the rocky ground.

The body bounced once and a little girl shrieked as she saw blood spurt from the crushed head. No one moved. No one said anything.

The police closed in. The fire engine came. The ambulance came. Finally the crowd dispersed. That evening the University announced postponement of any building plans for an indefinite period of time.

"We're all to blame," Sister Imelda said. "His blood is on our hands."

"Let's at least give him the respect of silence," Reginald said.

And, as it later turned out, all the Lollipops were in agreement that the incident was simply better not talked about.

8

By the first week of October school was well under way. Not so well under way that mid-semester exams were a threat or term papers more than a vague future worry. Just well enough under way so that everyone felt safe in not thinking about school at all.

It was a perfect time for revolution.

"A holy revolution is what we want," Reginald said to nobody. "What are we doing at Oak Road? How are we furthering the Thomasite ideal?"

He tapped his pencil against his desk and then against his forehead. After coffee tonight, before anyone could get away, he would confront them. But how do you confront a crowd like this? "God only knows," he said aloud, and then in a moment, "Only God knows." Purist, he thought.

But he would, by God, confront them. And tonight.

He tried again. "Why are we here? How are we living out the Thomasite ideal?"

Suddenly, in his mind, he saw them all get up and walk away.

What they were doing at Oak Road and how they were living out the Thomasite ideal were questions that would have baffled no one more than St. Gommer. That good man had thought long on the weakness of the flesh and had concluded that the only corrective was a change in the nature of humanity itself. Such a universal change was impossible and so he devised for his particular Thomasites what he considered the next best thing: a training process so prolonged and inflexible that when it was completed the Thomasite would never be the same again.

The process would take fourteen years. Holy and learned men, St. Gommer's first disciples, would receive into their bosoms the aspiring Thomasites and while they trained the intellect in every known field of human science, they would train the spirit in the virtues of charity and humility, train the will in absolute obedience.

Total formation, St. Gommer had called it, and for centuries it was to remain so. Thus Reginald and George and Hans, more than they guessed, were the products of the finest minds of the seventeenth century.

And indeed the traditional Thomasite training was impressive.

After a battery of exams which tested the candidate's physical and intellectual qualifications, and after a series of psychological exams in which he was asked many likely and some startling questions about moral attitudes and sex and habits, the successful applicant entered the Thomasites as a novice religious. For two years he was taught the history and ascetical principles of the order along with the fundamentals of prayer. If, at the end of these two years, he proved himself worthy—and anyone who remained, did—he was allowed to make his vows of poverty, chastity, and obedience as a Thomasite.

During this preparatory time discipline was severe and self-discipline was as complete as the novice could endure without "cracking his head," as Gommer and the psychology of his day put it. Communication of any kind was discouraged; only necessary conversation was allowed and that had to be in Latin; letters might be written only once a week, generally to parents.

Reginald had written home about the monastery and the lake and the beauties of living in the country, not acknowledging even to himself that he was miserable, that he missed the city, that he detested the wilderness. Hans had written about the monastery and the life of prayer and the beauties of living among saintly men, and he believed it, because he willed it to be so. But at this point in their career all novices wrote the same thing: they were happy and they loved God.

After these two bucolic years of religious life, the Thomasite novice made his vows and was called a scholastic—a religious who was not yet a priest and whose time was dedicated to his scholastic studies, when he was not at prayer, of course. For two years he immersed himself in the Latin and Greek classics and for three more in philosophy and science. This five-year exposure to learning was heady stuff and most Thomasites never recovered from it.

"My vows having been taken," Billy Biggins wrote to his mother, "and the novitiate period of religious formation being all done, I and the other novices have begun our classical studies, which is a lot harder than just grammar."

"Catullus," George wrote to his lovely cousin Alice, "is the dessert, but glorious Vergil is the meal."

Sean wrote few letters, but sporadically he kept a diary. "Detest Latin," he wrote. "Greek is even worse. Am reading *The Prancing Nigger* on the sly."

"The finger of God is everywhere—*cf.* Eclogue IV, Vergil," Hans wrote to his mother, a woman who could read no Latin and, indeed, managed English with considerable difficulty.

Reginald had become aware that he was miserable and didn't write at all.

During the three years of philosophy and science they all seemed to find themselves, all except Reginald, who grew more charming as he grew more miserable. But for the others, these years were pivotal.

George did an interpretation of matter and form in Aristotle and began a life of word study that would finally win him his Ph.D. from the University, though secretly word studies bored him to death.

Sean gave up trying to understand St. Thomas and turned to writing poetry full time. He had little talent for it but it preserved his sanity, or so he liked to say years later when, in his crazy chef's hat, he went weekly before the television cameras to demonstrate the preparation of gourmet dinners.

Hans, who had dutifully committed to memory all the Thomistic revelations on being and non-being, intellection of men and animals, matter and form of the universe, and who insisted upon discussing these with Professor O'Neil as if they were negotiable ideas, was finally told by that short-tempered priest that he ought to go study history. Hans took this for the sign he had awaited and thereafter threw his limitless energies into the study of history, where in fact he was supremely happy.

And Billy Biggins, who had never done well at anything, finally placed first in one of his classes, Tests and Measurements, and so launched himself on a career in counseling psychology where he did little harm, since soon after his ordination he was made a Superior and remained one all his life.

Three years of teaching followed the long years of classics, philosophy, and science. Scholastics were dispatched to the many schools of the Order and there taught a heavy load of classes in subjects Superiors thought them suited for; in addition, they directed the school plays, edited the newspaper and the yearbook, coached sports, and sometimes functioned as janitors. It was in this period of teaching that Reginald most widely exercised his charm, George discovered the distinct attraction of girls, and Hans, whose students shrieked at him both in the classroom and on the ballfield, found ample opportunities to exercise his will.

It was in this period of teaching that Sean and Billy and Jim now found themselves, though in their cases the teaching period was given over to further study in their special fields, a practice which Thomasite adaptation was making more and more common.

Four years of theology culminated in ordination, after which the active Thomasite life began. The new priest, if he had not yet finished his doctoral degree, did so now, and then was assigned to the missions or to the colleges or, if he were difficult, to one of the Order's expensive preparatory schools that dotted the wooded areas of Massachusetts and Connecticut.

It was a rich and comprehensive course which marked the man forever a Thomasite. His thinking, his work, his behavior, even his unconscious reactions to people and events would always remain conditioned by these fourteen years of training for the priesthood, though it had always been true that in many cases the conditioning resulted in the opposite of what had been intended. Thus, the lapsed Thomasite was often rich, unchaste, and a rebel, with a positive disdain for the intellectual life. Either way, the formation was total and the Thomasite course of studies was impressive.

Renowned for their intellect and their doubt, with a long history of inflexible ideals and pragmatic adaptations, the Thomasites were the first to adapt, update, to implement the decrees of Vatican II. Indeed, even before the Council was convened, plans were afoot to remove the theological students from the forests and place them on the campus of the University.

The fame of the Order and the distinction of the Thomasite teaching faculty were items not lost on Dr. Thumbell, Dean of the University's Divinity School, nor had he failed to consider the forty thousand rare books in the Thomasite study halls. When Father Superior had approached him and pointed out that a sharing of faculties and libraries might be to the advantage of both the Order and the University, Dr. Thumbell had darted his tongue back and forth between his thin lips and said, yes, yes, he would propose it; yes, yes, it was not unwarranted; the Thomasites, of course, so many outstanding scholars; and he had gone on for some time in fear and delight at what the consequences of his proposal might be.

The University accepted the idea of a merger, and on to its campus came the Thomasite theological faculty and a large selection of Thomasite students who would henceforth receive their degrees from the Divinity School. There was one awful drawback Dr. Thumbell had carelessly overlooked. Preparation for the priesthood meant certain obligatory courses, and thus the University found itself in the peculiar position of offering lectures in Canon Law and Moral Theology to a student body that had suddenly become two-thirds Roman Catholic. The founding fathers would have wept.

Certainly the more conservative Thomasites wept. And yet, though they mourned the evil day and predicted worse to come, the move to the University campus had been a profitable one. The Thomasites had bought two old rooming houses on Winter Place and at a cost of a quarter-million dollars had joined them, gutted the upper stories, and fitted them out for thirty theological students. At this point in the business Rome gave its belated approval to the move, but insisted that at least ten older wiser priests be assigned to Winter Place, "to afford spiritual consolation to the younger men and, by the holiness of their lives, offer contrast to the hedonistic ideals of the secular University." A quick search failed to turn up ten such men—the retirees were either impossible to live with or were too far gone in alcohol—and so the rooms were given to Thomasite graduate students, even though it was generally acknowledged that they were a much more harmful influence on the young men than the University itself. Still, the letter of Rome's command was observed and that was all that mattered.

For seven years, then, the old house on Winter Place had been the center of Thomasite theological studies and a home for graduate students as well. It was clean and comfortable and close to all the University buildings. Further, it was ruled by Father Sheehey, a benign old priest of great tolerance, whose only passion was the celebration of feasts.

Father Sheehey had been surprised when some of the boys had decided to leave Winter Place and set up house on Oak Road. Think of the inconvenience. Think of the boredom, with only five of them around. They wanted a small community. Well, maybe small communities were the thing of the future, who was he to say? And God knows the Thomasites had always led the way into the future. First the Council, then the University, why not Oak Road?

He shrugged and smiled and shook his head.

Though, the more you thought about it, what on earth *were* they doing at Oak Road?

He wished them well.

"While we're all here," Reginald said, "there's something we've got to talk about."

Everyone put down coffee cups; Reg had that tone in his voice again.

"I mean, I've been doing a lot of thinking about this and

I think we ought to talk about it. It's about time we decided exactly what we're doing here."

There was a moment of imcomprehension. Even Sean said nothing.

"We're Thomasites and we're priests, two of us are priests, and we're living in this place. What I'm trying to say is this: What are we doing here?"

"We're giving witness to Christ and to others," Hans said immediately. He could have been reading from notes. "By our vows we give witness to Christ that we put Him ahead of all worldly wealth and ahead of the sinful pleasures of the flesh and ahead of our own self will. By our lives we give witness to other people that their lives are materialistic and selfish." He finished and looked around, pleased.

Sean applauded. "Jesus Christ," he said and, piling his plates rapidly, he scuffed back his chair and went into the kitchen.

"We did all that in the novitiate," Billy said, puzzled.

Reginald shook his head and looked down the table at Jim. The situation was impossible. Jim returned his look and smiled with one corner of his mouth.

"What do *you* think we're doing here?" Jim said.

"Well, I thought we could at least talk about it." Reginald realized that the chance to talk had already escaped him.

"It's what I said," Hans insisted. "We give witness to Christ and to others. By our vows . . ."

"So talk," Jim said to Reginald. They both ignored Hans who continued to recite anyway.

"What do *you* think?" Reginald said.

"I think we're here to be professionals."

Reginald thought a moment. "Professionals? You mean professional priests? What do you mean?"

"No. We're here to be priests, *by* being professionals. "That's how I fulfill my priesthood, by being a doctor."

"You're joking," Reginald said.

"I'm a priest first and always," Hans said. "That's the whole point of being a Thomasite. First a priest, second a Thomasite, and then, and only then, a doctor. Or, in my case a scholar."

"You're joking," Reginald said to Jim.

"I'm dead serious," Hans began, "I'm a priest first . . ."

"I don't see the problem," Billy said. "I don't see what the problem is."

"Can it," Reginald said. And to Jim, "Are you serious that you think you fulfill your priesthood by being a doctor?"

"Of course." Jim was amused at Reginald's astonishment.

"Then why not be just a doctor and forget the priesthood altogether? Or why not be a disc jockey or a garbage collector? Jesus!" He was beginning to get angry at such radical notions.

"Because," Jim said patiently, "I prefer to be a doctor. I also like the idea of being a priest. And if priesthood means service, then I'll serve by being a doctor."

"*You* think the priesthood is some kind of club. You think it's something you belong to on weekends or on national holidays."

"Isn't it?"

"That's incredible. That's outrageous."

"Oh God. Even you?" Jim gathered his dishes, saying as he left the room, "Beware the departmental mind, Reg. It could swallow you up forever."

"Why did he say that?" Billy asked. "We wouldn't get anywhere without the departmental mind. Heavens!"

"People like that shouldn't be allowed to get ordained," Hans said. "What kind of witness can you give if you think it's all right to be a doctor first and a priest second? We ought to discuss this and make a report to Father Superior."

"Time for dishes," Reginald said, sorry he had begun the discussion in the first place.

Late that night he found that he was still disturbed by what Jim had said. You've got to have faith, he told himself. Everything's going to be okay, but you've got to believe.

He decided to say the Rosary. He had not said the Rosary in several years and by the third decade he was surprised how meaningless it seemed, the long succession of Hail Mary's, the sacred mysteries that kept slipping out of mind. Better to finish, though. Always finish anything you've begun, especially if it goes against the grain.

Why am I doing this, he thought, counting out the fiftieth Hail Mary.

"Why not?" he said aloud. And having said that, he went to the kitchen and poured himself a double jigger of scotch.

9

"Why?" Natalie said.

"Why not?" he said. "Come on to bed."

"There's more to life than just sex, George. There's ideas for one thing. And there are books and people. And for goodness sake, there's music. You always used to like music."

"Come on to bed. We'll make music."

"Oh, George. That's so corny."

"Come on," he said, naked and erect, after a fashion.

Reginald met Bob Moran and Sister Imelda, as they had planned, at Logan airport. They were flying to Washington for the Moratorium to express, along with thousands of others, their discontent with the Vietnam War. The lounge overflowed with young people laughing, calling back and forth to one another, and with older people, who stood or sat, often in family groups, a little pleased with themselves for what they were about to do.

"Hi," Reginald said, flashing that smile.

Sister Imelda looked at him, thin and muscular in his chinos and white windbreaker, and her heart sank. With his blond hair and light skin, with all those white and tan clothes, it wasn't fair; he looked like an ice-cream cone.

"Hey, you're not wearing your veil," he said.

"No, veils are out," she said. "If we don't wear habits,

we shouldn't wear veils. Besides, it was an awful nuisance."

"Good," he said. "That's fine." He noticed also that she had done something about the hair on her upper lip, that suggestion of a moustache which for months he had forced himself not to stare at, had now disappeared. She looked, in fact, almost pretty.

"I feel more like a woman," she said, gazing at him, despairing.

"How about a drink?" Bob Moran felt protective about Sister Imelda and was embarrassed to see her throwing herself at Reginald.

Actually, Sister Imelda would have been astonished at such a thought. What interested her was the Movement, priests and nuns working together as human beings for the underprivileged, for peace, for the Church. She had given up her life, or at least ten years of it, for these ideals. That some man—even someone as personally attractive as Reginald—might siphon off her vital spiritual energies was preposterous. Reginald interested her only because he was a fine priest and a gentle one; he could be so easily hurt or taken advantage of. And there were too many, even in the Movement, who were willing to take advantage of him. One of her hopes was to protect him from these people, to be a shield, a blanket for him. She looked at him and tried without success to dismiss the thought that he was an ice-cream cone.

"Oh, a drink!" she said. "Terrif!" And with her slightly masculine walk she strode off to Cloud Nine, Logan's cocktail lounge.

"Hey, Father, can we use your side of the cellar for a clubhouse? You guys don't use it."

"Well, I don't know," Hans said. He sat on the porch stairs next to Francis, pleased that he had real rapport with kids. "What kind of club do you have?"

"Just a club. You know, sort of like the Boy Scouts," Michael said.

"Oh, the Boy Scouts."

"Well, not really the Boy Scouts." Francis was more sophisticated in these, as in other, matters. "It's sort of an Irish Club. But for Americans. It's patriotic." Hans, he knew, was not a Communist.

Hans liked the sound of that, and when he finally understood that they could enter the cellar from a door on their own side of the house, he told them yes, certainly, and asked what they called their club.

"The White Eagles," they said together.

And so on Friday evening, when the family was out shopping for groceries, Francis taught fat Judy Molocha a thing or two he had picked up from *Portnoy's Complaint* while Michael, impressed, indeed terrified, crouched behind the Thomasites' trunks, watching.

> "I hoped to send you something nice
> A small bijou, champagne on ice,
> A nothing bought at Lord and Taylor . . ."

What rhymes with Taylor, Sean thought. Sailor, frailer, paler. He was working on a verse for his sister's birthday.

Thomasites didn't give presents and he hated cards—if you care enough to send the very best, you don't send a crappy card, he had said—and so every year for each of his two sisters and two brothers, he ground out a few rhymes. They were no trouble, taking only a few minutes to write, and sometimes he even enjoyed them.

An autograph from Norman Mailer? No, better change the store. Peck & Peck.

"A nothing bought at Peck & Peck
Or, failing that, a modest check
Made out to Shreve and Crump and Low
To celebrate your birth, you know.
I thought about things sane and whacky
Ari likes to buy for Jackie,
And then about my lack of wealth
To buy you furs, to toast your health
At Antoine's, or even at the Ritz."

Ritz. Ritz. It was so easy, so stupid.

"An when I'd nearly lost my wits,
I . . ."

I what? Sean sat looking at the paper. Everything had just tumbled out and now he was at a standstill. He doodled. He tilted back in his chair and studied the Magritte print that hung above his desk. Poetry was a mystery, that's for damned sure, but never before had doggerel slipped so completely from him. He took a fresh piece of paper and wrote in his spidery hand:

"There was an old card shark out West
Whose genitals grew from his chest."

No, that wasn't going to be any help. What he needed, he decided, was a tranquilizer, but by some awful carelessness on his part, he was out of them. He began to panic. It was too early to begin drinking. Desperate, he went to the kitchen where he baked a peach strudel, a secret recipe he had inherited from his German grandmother.

"What? What do you want?" Natalie said, her voice husky with sleep.

George shook her gently and kissed her neck, meanwhile moving his body against hers.

"Come on," he said.

"Oh, not again, George. No."

"Come on," he said, and his hand slid from her small perfect breasts down the curve of her ribs and waist. She brought her knees up sharply to his groin. George yelped in pain.

"Oh, George, I'm sorry," she said. "It was an accident, really," and then she laughed softly.

"Come on now, cut it out," he said, all business, and slipped his hand between her legs.

"Sometimes I think you think love and sex are the same thing," Natalie said.

George stiffened all over. It had never occurred to him, that, at least as far as living was concerned, there was any difference. In fiction, of course, you made a distinction.

10

I'm becoming a narcissist, George said to himself, combing his eyebrows with an old toothbrush. He was trying to make them slant up in the middle instead of just lying flat in a line across his forehead. Combed up, they emphasized his eyes, his best feature, a velvety brown color now that he had switched from plain contact lenses to violet-tinted ones. He blinked rapidly at himself and made big eyes. I am, he said, and smiled at the mirror with his long teeth. Damn, they were yellowish, no getting away from it.

He stepped back to take in the whole picture. Tall, trim, good looking. At thirty-five he still had no pot and his Air Force exercises had kept his muscles firm. He turned in profile, sucking in his belly. His new hip-hugging trousers were right for him, he thought, tight in the crotch so that he displayed a fine masculine bulge. He tipped his pelvis forward and up. "Cock," he said aloud, "Fuck." He was trying to rid himself of the false modesty acquired during all those years of Thomasite training. "Fuck," he said again and then, remembering his plans for the evening, said, "My Jesus, mercy."

George had decided that he must break with Natalie, this time for good. For one thing he was running out of confessors; they all told him the same thing anyhow, that he must break with the girl. Besides, he was not ready to leave the priesthood. He liked being a priest and he had to finish his degree before he could even consider leaving. So better end things with Natalie now.

He laid the toothbrush on the bureau next to his coin caddy, thought a moment, and then put it in the top drawer. He liked plain flat surfaces and could never understand why other Thomasites heaped their bureaus and desk tops with bottles and brushes and papers. What did they think drawers were for? They, in turn, joked about his compulsive neatness and referred to his room, at least among themselves, as the bridal suite.

His room was larger than the others—a technical accident of the reconstruction—and he had taken pains to find matching drapes and bedspread. Some thousand books dominated one wall; the number at first had astonished Father Sheehey but George explained at length that English literature, and especially his highly technical branch of English literature, made owning so many books an absolute necessity. Father Sheehey had heard such things before; he nodded and went away. The books had, in fact, played a large part in George's decision not to move to Oak Road. The very thought of moving them made him tired.

And then there were his *objets*. On a small bookcase between the windows, indeed the focal point for anyone entering the room, he had arranged the possessions he considered most valuable or most interesting. A crystal paperweight by Steuben, an original Beardsley drawing, small but genuine, a silver dagger from Baghdad, several leather-framed photographs of students and a gold-framed one of his mother—these were his *objets*. "Nothings, really; just little—well, *objets*." And with them, conspicuously, was a small lacquered box with a hinged lid carved by hand in India; inside he kept a collection of ticket stubs from his London trip, proof that he had been to Anne Hathaway's cottage, the Abbey, the Tower, and an astonishing number of plays. "You've never seen theatre until you've seen London theatre." He had no ticket stubs from Paris or Rome or Vienna, though he had spent time in all of them. He had skied in the Alps ("exhilarating, really"), swum in the Mediterranean ("there are still a few patches of good beach"), and carried on flirtations everywhere he stayed for more than a day and sometimes on the trains getting there. George had been assigned to do his theological studies in Europe and, by telling his German Superiors that he had permission from Boston and his Boston Superiors he had German permission, he managed an unprecedented amount of travel. He justified his distortion of the facts by reminding himself that it was folly to be in Europe and not use it. George, more than any Thomasite before him, had used Europe, as the *objets* of the bridal suite testified.

He looked around now, nervous, and with a final tweak to his tie, he set off for Natalie's.

But at the corner of Winter Place and Irving Street, there was Natalie herself. She wore a short black skirt and a heavy black sweater and she looked sad.

"Natalie!" His tone was uncertain; he did not like being seen with girls in public.

"Hello, George."

"But I thought we had a date."

"We do, in a way." She knew what a date meant.

"In a way?"

"In a way. We're together but we're not going to bed."

"*Not* going."

"Not going. To bed. That's all over with, George." She sounded very definite; it was not like Natalie.

"Let's talk about it," he said and turned in the direction of her apartment.

"We're not going there, George."

"We've got to go somewhere. We can't talk like this right here in the middle of the street."

"There's nothing to say, George. I just want to end it. The whole thing has been a mistake."

"Come on, we'll talk about it."

"No, George."

"Come on."

She saw it was hopeless. "Tell you what, George," she said. "You can buy me a beer at the Wursthaus." At least he couldn't carry on much there.

"Too public. Let's go to your place."

"Too private. How about Dumfey's? We can get a beer there. It's Dumfey's or nothing, George."

"Dumfey's" he said.

"That's a good George. That's a good Georgie," she said, infuriating him with her tone.

They walked in silence for a while, two scholars thinking out a solution to an especially perplexing problem.

Natalie was pleased. She had determined earlier in the week that on Friday she would tell George the affair was over. She had never had an affair before and she did not like this one. In her senior year at Columbia she had moved in with a math major; they were in love and would have married had it not been for Natalie's insistence that they wait until she was certain of her own mind. She had never arrived at the necessary certitude and so at graduation, when he accepted a scholarship to Stanford and she accepted one to the University, they had simply parted. But she did not consider that an affair; that had been love, mutual and honest. The business with George was an affair.

George was not pleased. His pride was hurt. He had planned on ending the affair himself, and as a man and a priest it was his right to do so. What ever could have gotten into her to explain this new wrongheadedness? It wasn't like her. Furthermore, he had planned on breaking the news to her early the next morning, after another athletic night of love. Guiltily, he looked around to see if they were being observed. In the months with Natalie he had never once taken her out in the evening. Lunches were all right, everyone had lunch with girls, but a date, a real planned going-out-together date was unthinkable for a priest. The whole situation was infuriating. Why did she want to break off anyway.

"Why do you want to break off, anyway?"

"It's not right."

"What do you mean, it's not right?"

"It's not moral."

"Not moral! Not moral!"

People passing in the Quad turned to stare at the couple.

"Oh my God," he said, whispering.

"Don't worry, they'll think we're talking about the war."

He was dumb with outrage. *She* telling *him* it was not moral. *She* telling *him*. A *priest*. He was about to say this when he realized the vulnerability of his position and, after a struggle, said nothing.

"It's not moral," she said, "because we're not in love."

"What on earth does love have to do with it! Sin is sin. Love doesn't make it right. If it's not moral, it's because it's sinful, period. Not because we're not in love." For a bright girl, she could be terribly opaque.

"I don't know what you learn in your theology books, George, I'm just telling you why it's not moral to me."

"To me, to me! There you are again. Morality isn't relative. A thing is right or wrong no matter what any given individual thinks about it."

"Is fornication moral?"

"It's *not* moral!"

"Good, George, that was my point. If it was love, that would be another matter. But with us it was only fornication."

George was silent, uncertain whether he had won his point. Frustrated, furious, he wanted only one thing: to go to bed with her at once.

But by this time they were at the battered wooden door of Dumfey's.

Dumfey's had been the University hangout in the days when hangouts had flourished; now, like all such places, it had fallen upon hard times. The sawdust floor and the barracky atmosphere remained, but what had once been a place for intellectuals to go slumming was now just a place to go slumming. The forty booths had high thick walls and the tables could seat as many as ten or twelve and so Dumfey's was popular with revolutionaries of every stripe. The SDS met there, the more social members of Weatherman, the Black Panthers, the Lollipops, and there was always a token representation from the FBI.

As George held the door for her, Natalie peered into all the visible booths; surely she would know somebody here.

"We've got to see it scripturally, I say. Christ said, 'I've come to set brother against brother,' so I don't see what's wrong with explosives."

"I think Doris has a point." Sister Gunnekild leaned on the Doris.

"No, no, no," Bob Moran said. "Violence is always . . ."

"Bob, what a nice thing to see you." Natalie had spotted Bob Moran who, like George, had been in her Middle English class.

Bob was stunned. He knew everyone and everyone knew him, but it was always he who made the initial approach. And suddenly here stood Natalie, beautiful, smiling. He began to get red.

"Do you know my friend, George St. George?" she said, determined not to be alone with him.

"We've been studying," George said.

"Everyone knows George." Bob was grinning insanely. Natalie Meyer!

"Everyone," Natalie said, turning to the miserable George.

"Oh, I'm forgetting my . . . this is Sister Gunnekild, Natalie Meyer. She's in English. Sister is in, um, Religious Studies. And this is Sister Imelda."

"Doris," she corrected. "I used to be Sister Imelda, but I've gone back to my name. Doris Hanlon. But I'm still a Sister."

"And this is Reginald. You know Reginald, don't you?"

"No, but I'm pleased . . ."

"No, but I'm pleased . . ."

They spoke together and then laughed together and, as Reginald kept looking at Natalie and smiling, Doris put a sisterly hand on his arm, a proprietary gesture not lost to any of them.

When the introductions were over, there was nothing that could be done except ask them to stay and have a beer. Doomed, George sat watching the ebullient Natalie dazzle Bob Moran and, for all he knew, the rest of the table.

"We shouldn't interrupt," she said and took a dainty swig of her beer. "What were you all talking about?"

"We, uh . . ."

"We."

"We were talking about whether or not it's Christian to bomb buildings," Reginald said, and laughed as if it were meant to be a joke. The others stared at him aghast.

"Christians are so moral," Natalie said, and her laughter rippled in a way George had never noticed. He thought of taking her by force here at the table. "So *consciously* moral." And she laughed again.

Reginald laughed too, and there they were, both of them laughing when nothing funny had been said. George was furious. Sister Imelda, née Doris, was furious. The others felt confused, as if they had missed the point of a joke. Bob Moran felt deserted; after all Natalie was, in a way, his guest.

By midnight they had all drunk a great deal of beer, and walking home in their several groups each one felt obliged to clarify the evening, to summarize it in a single point, a relic perhaps of their religious training.

"Too bad outsiders came."

"I don't know, Sister, she . . ."

"Doris. Not Sister. Doris."

"Doris. She seemed like a very intelligent girl to me. Don't you think so, Bob?"

"She is. Yes," Bob said, trying not to watch as Doris slipped her hand through Reginald's arm. She squeezed against him for a second and gave a little giggle. Reginald only blinked once or twice and stared straight ahead. He looked as if he were gritting his teeth.

"I'll walk you home and we'll talk about it."

"No, George. There's nothing to talk about."

"I'll walk you home."

"You're not going to come in, George."

"We'll talk about it."

She might shake him off at Dumfey's but, by God, she wouldn't get away with it at her apartment.

Sister Gunnekild shared a suite with Doris in the Women's Dorm. Having once been instructed by Doris that the walk home with Reginald was a great spiritual consolation, and a personal one as well, she never interfered again. She was escorted home this evening by two anonymous Christian Brothers.

"I don't go for bombing," one said.

"What about the FBI?" the other said.

"Is she Jewish? If she's Jewish, she'd be ideal for the Lollipops." Sister Gunnekild always wore a pin that said "I give a damn."

"She must be Jewish. Meyer."

"Now if we could only get a black," she said.

"What about George?"

"George isn't black. What are you talking about?"

"For the Lollipops, I mean, what about George?"

"No, not George. All George cares about is books."

"Goodnight, Reg." Bob was desperate to get away.

"Goodnight, Reggie." Doris gave his arm an extra little squeeze.

"I don't like that," Reginald said.

Doris let go of his arm.

"Don't do that," Reginald said. "I don't like being pawed and I don't like being possessed."

Doris made a sound as if she were trying to catch her breath.

At the stairs Reginald turned and said in an altogether different voice, a calm voice, as if nothing had happened, "Goodnight, now. Peace."

Everyone knew Reg was a thinker, but no one had guessed he was so definite. Bob thought about this as he and Doris walked for some time in silence. Reg was a deep one all right.

"Reg is touchy," she said finally. "I think Reg works too hard. It's the new house and everything."

Bob said nothing.

"He's worried about the Lollipops too," she said. "If he feels that strongly about bombing, I for one am willing to give it up."

Still Bob said nothing.

"He's tired," she said. "That's all it is, he's tired." Finally she could not help herself. "Well, what do *you* think?"

"I think he doesn't like the way you throw yourself at him."

"That's crazy," she said immediately. "That's ridiculous."

"And I think he's right."

Bob said no more. Nor did Doris, though she studied him carefully each time they passed a streetlight. She had begun to worry that he was right, for she knew Bob had an eye for such things.

"Good night, George."

"Let me come in for just a minute."

"No, George."

"I have something I want to say."

"Not a chance, George."

"You don't love me."

"I'm sorry, but that's true."

"You never did."

"I thought I did."

"I love you," he said accusingly and pressed his body against hers.

"That's not love, George. That's just guilt you're waiting to savor."

He pinned her arms against her side and pressed his mouth on hers, thrusting his pelvis hard against her. But she wriggled far enough away to knee him expertly, if lightly, in the groin, and in his momentary panic she slipped into her apartment and locked the door.

"Thank God," she said, although she did not believe in God.

George decided it would be unbecoming to pound at her door. He squared his shoulders and hitched up his trousers. He would retire, at any rate, with his dignity intact.

The fifteen-minute walk back to Winter Place gave him time to sort out his feelings: he was frustrated sexually at not having slept with her, he was wounded spiritually that she had ended the affair before he did, and he had a pain in the balls. He sat in the bridal suite wondering what would become of him. He liked sex; it was not his fault that he had come to it so late. He liked women, though the only one he knew was Natalie. How had he ever gotten to be a priest in the first place?

He began seriously to turn this question over in his mind. But immediately, in Thomasite fashion, innumerable other questions lined up behind that one. Should he have become a priest? Should he remain one? Shouldn't he, if he had a shred of honesty left, shouldn't he get out? Didn't he, in fact, want to get out? Wasn't it only his uncompleted degree . . . ?

He shook his head violently to dispel the whole unpleasant subject. He considered masturbating, but that was so boring he had to be terribly drunk to bother. A drink.

Two hours later George was still sitting on his bed drinking scotch. Scattered around him were ticket stubs for Anne Hathaway's cottage, the Tower of London, the Royal Crypt at Westminster Abbey, ballet tickets, concert tickets, tickets for trains and tours and theatres—all proof of something that eluded him for the moment.

Everything had gone so wrong—all the ideals scattered. He pushed the ticket stubs aside and picked up the silver dagger from Baghdad. He slipped it out of its scabbard. The blade appeared to be silver too but must be steel, of course. Running his finger over the razor edge, he walked to the mirror and placed the tip of the knife at his throat. He pressed it slightly and a small point of red appeared on his flesh.

He stood there for a full minute and then for another, the knife at his throat, the hand that held it trembling only slightly. And then tears leaped to his eyes and he lowered the knife.

"Not old George," he said grimly. "Old George is going to survive."

11

Toward the end of 1699 St. Gommer found himself afflicted by that discomfort and suspicion with which wise men always greet a new century. There were portents of disaster—seven Bishops had given up their mistresses within the same week, it had rained blood in a small village in southern France, and in Boulogne a child had been born with the face of a poodle—but these Gommer dismissed as popular panic. His own panic was of a different sort.

In 1699, in a moment of clearsightedness that amounted to a vision, St. Gommer beheld the possibility of a whole new class of men, a fourth class.

St. Gommer's writings on the three classes of men were already a staple of ascetic literature. The first class included those who saw the goal, saw the steps to the goal, and took them. This was a rarified class and Gommer called its members Saints. The second class, larger in number, included those who saw the goal and the steps to it, but who took only some of the steps, their major efforts spent on looking after themselves. These he called Survivors. The third class was mankind at large. These men saw the goal, saw that the steps to it were too difficult, and forgot about the enterprise altogether. He called them the Savable.

The possibility of a fourth class unnerved Gommer considerably and he took to his bed. This new class, this fourth class of men about which he himself never wrote, he called the Clang Birds.

St. Gommer greeted the year 1700 with a frown.

12

In his dream Reginald saw the hill just ahead and told himself that in one second he would look over his shoulder and see where Weidecker was. Meanwhile, the macadam slipped away beneath him and he ran joyously, his head high. In his dream victory was certain, the race itself was all punishment and pleasure. Reginald was running for the hundredth time the race he had won by a spectacular margin some twenty years earlier.

On that morning they were racing Central High. Buddy Cosgrove took one look at the opposition and was rendered helpless by diarrhea; he had heard a lot about Weidecker, the captain, who had never lost a race, but he was not prepared for the sight of him. Huge, with massive shoulders and chest, Weidecker was not built like any runner Buddy had ever seen, but his thighs and calfs were the giveaway. They looked like steel and probably were. Buddy's insides crumbled and he made a dash for the locker room.

The coach shrugged—what can you do?—and though Reginald was new to the team and had not run with it before, the coach put him in Cosgrove's place.

"Do your best," he said, and as an afterthought, "just try not to come in last."

Reginald knew he would lose, but he hoped that by keeping up with the second-class runners he would finish, anonymously, in a crowd.

Tensed in a crouch, he shot a glance at Weidecker. Why go second class? Keep with Weidecker, Reginald told himself. Keep as close as possible for as long as you can, so that when you fall back. . . .

The whistle blew. The two teams sprinted furiously, despite the fact that this was a two-mile course and they had been ordered over and over again to pace themselves. Very soon the pack slowed down and four boys moved steadily out front, Weidecker leading, Reginald three paces behind, and two boys from Central breathing heavily at Reginald's heels. He felt wonderful. At least he would not finish last.

When they reached the mile turn, he and Weidecker had

hanging down. Weidecker was grinning and his legs were pumping hard. Slowly, mercilessly, he was gaining on Reginald.

For the first time in his dream Reginald wondered if he would win, if he could win. He fixed his eyes on the finish line and ran furiously, with the fury of desperation.

13

"He's charming," Sean said.

"Who?" Billy said.

"Reg. Good old Reg. He's charming."

Reginald had just left the living room where he had been watching television with Sean and Billy and Hans. As he passed behind Sean, he had rumpled his hair.

"But men aren't charming," Billy said, "only women are charming."

"Who says?"

"Because that's how it is. That's what the word means."

"The word 'charm,' my good man, means to please, to fascinate, to cast a spell. If there is anyone we know who fascinates, it's Reg."

Billy looked puzzled. Hans leaned forward and cupped

his ear, the better to hear the television.

"He's got that smile," Sean continued, "and all those white teeth. They drive people crazy. Look at the people who follow him around over at the University. Look at us, for crying out loud. The real reason any of us are here is because Reg was at the bottom of the plan."

"Ha!" Hans said, continuing to stare at the television.

"And why? When you talk, he listens. When you suffer, he aches. He's gorgeous. He's a young John Lindsay. He should run for President. He should run for God."

"You're talking about me again." Jim had come in on the tail of Sean's eulogy. "If nominated, I will not run. If elected, I will not serve."

"Balls, oh doctor," Sean said.

Hans stormed from the room muttering, "a house of prayer, ha, a house of religion." The others ignored him.

"We were talking about old Reg," Sean explained. "I was trying to convince Billy that Reg is loaded with charisma."

"Of course he is. He's professionally charming. That's the nature of his priesthood," Jim said.

"Charming. You see?" Sean turned to Billy. "Exactly my my point. Reg is charming."

"*Professionally* charming," Jim said.

"Well, I still think it's a word you only apply to women," Billy insisted.

"You're right," Jim said. "To women—and to priests."

Jim turned and left. Billy and Sean sat in silence before the television set, each thinking very different thoughts.

14

Christmas wreaths hung on both doors of the duplex and candles stood in the four front windows. The Thomasites had plain white lights, or rather Reginald had them since it was his windows they illumined. The McReedys had red ones which blinked on and off every half-minute. A Christmas tree, slumping under pounds of lights which also blinked on and off, blazed in the McReedy front window. The curtains were kept open and the shades kept up to share the sight with all of Oak Road.

The McReedys loved Christmas and celebrated it with Irish abandon. "We go all out for Christmas," Officer McReedy liked to say at headquarters, "money is no objective; we go all out." And so they did.

The boys had long since observed that at Christmas their mother scolded only half as much, their father was home nights, except on weekends, and Grandma Shea was less of a pain in the ass. And, too, at Christmas they cleaned up on gifts. Though it was still a week until Christmas, they knew everything they would receive, having ransacked Grandma Shea's closet and, for larger gifts, the attic. Grandma Shea had bought Michael an erector set, an idea which caused Francis to roll his eyes and shriek like a maniac, saying Judy Molocha was *his* erector set. For Francis she had bought an elaborate outlay of chemistry equipment—test tubes, a Bunsen Burner, and a hundred little jars of harmless chemicals.

This pleased him greatly and set his fertile mind scheming.

This evening the boys sat beneath the tree, Officer McReedy on one side, the Mrs. on the other—he with a bottle of beer in his hand, she with the *Boston Globe* folded on her lap. Lawrence Welk blared from the television in the corner. A family scene, with Grandma Shea alone on the love seat.

"Home and family," Officer McReedy said. "Christmas."

Mrs. McReedy nodded agreement.

"Right, Ma?" he shouted at his mother-in-law. She was deaf and generally ignored, but this was the Christmas season.

"It's m'legs," she said, rubbing her knees.

"That's right, ma." He took a long swallow of his beer.

"Welk, Mary," he pointed to the television.

Mrs. McReedy nodded agreement.

"Good clean entertainment," he said, in the mood for conversation. "Like the old days. American."

It was the cue Francis had been waiting for.

"Dad, how come you don't arrest the Black Panthers for stomping me? How come?"

The question had arisen before, and repeatedly, until Francis had been forbidden to mention it again. Even now, at Christmas, the response was electric.

"Christ sakes, kid . . ."

"Fran, not in front of the boys."

"Christ, kid, you don't know what they're like, those Panthers. You can't just bust in on them and shoot them, you know. You got to have evidence. You got to have documents and reasonable grounds and all kinds of shit."

"Fran, not . . ."

"In Chicago they did. They shot this guy right in bed."

"Yeah, sure. But you've gotta be a goddam FBI man or something for that. If a plain cop did that they'd cut off his, uh, feet." He took another swallow of beer and turned back to the television set. He could feel his son staring at him. "So stop staring. Christ, I'd arrest them if I could. You're my kid. It's Christmas. But they got laws."

"I'm gonna get those niggers, Dad."

"Blacks. Jesus, kid, call them blacks. Your old man's a cop."

"I'm gonna get them."

"Yeah, you get them, that's right, you get them." And he added, addressing himself, "I wish to Christ somebody would dynamite the bastards."

"Fran, now." Mrs. McReedy rustled her paper at him. "Not while Joanne plays the piano."

They watched in silence while Joanne, filled with joy, bounced in her seat and waggled her platinum head as she thunked the piano keys. She was playing "Those Old Piano Roll Blues" and she smiled into the camera as the song rushed into another chorus, circular fashion, as if it might never end.

Mrs. McReedy shook her head sadly; sorrow had always been her response to talent. Officer McReedy, having sent Michael for another beer, now sat tapping his foot in time to the music, trying to put the Panthers far from his thoughts. Francis hated Joanne and her piano and for that matter Lawrence Welk, and so he lay on the floor thrusting his pelvis to the rhythm of the music. This unhinged Michael who was convulsed by sex whenever he was not appalled and he began to roll around the room with his fist in his mouth. Officer McReedy kicked his behind as it fell momentarily within range. Only Grandma Shea did not turn to face the television. She rubbed her arthritic knees and, hypnotized by the blinking lights, looked straight ahead at the Christmas tree. She knew it was folly—her eyes were beginning to cross—but there was nothing she could do about it.

At last a television commercial intervened and Joanne, her smile frozen, bowed at the McReedys.

"Why can't you dynamite them?"

"Dynamite who?"

"The Panthers. You said you wished somebody would dynamite the bastards, so why don't you? Why don't the police?"

Mrs. McReedy, who enjoyed commercials, looked up at "bastard." "Frankie," she said, "don't ever use that word."

"You use it. Dad uses it."

"And don't be fresh. You're getting too fresh sometimes. I'll speak to Father O'Boyle about you." She returned to the commercial.

"Well, why don't you? They use dynamite, why don't you?"

"Because there are laws, I already told you. Cut the shit now. No more, or you go up to bed."

They all watched the television while a man in a tuxedo tap-danced. Officer McReedy was disgusted; he didn't like to see men dance, it was faggoty, but given the situation, he pretended interest.

"Anyway, get me a beer," he said, and that, so far as he was concerned, ended the discussion.

The discussion was not ended; Francis had merely postponed his inquiry.

As he sat on the floor with his brother, the model of a child chastised, Francis' thoughts flickered brightly between his chemistry set and the new exciting possibilities of dynamite. He was glad his father was a cop.

15

By comparison with the McReedy's electrical extravaganza, the Thomasites might have been in mourning. Reginald had bought the two little candles that stood in his bedroom windows only as a concession to the neighbors. This he was willing to do, and no more.

He had always disliked the Thomasite fuss over Christmas decorations, the weeks of twining laurel into long streamers, the cutting and pasting of angels and Santa Clauses and five-pointed stars. Even as a novice he had half suspected these were artificial enthusiasms deliberately whipped up by Superiors to make the Thomasites feel they were all kids again, pure of heart, innocent of emotion, waiting for the big day which would end their misery.

No more of it for me, Reginald told himself, and he told the others that if they wanted a Christmas tree, they'd better look after it themselves. No one said anything, but they exchanged surprised looks. There were moments these days when Reginald wasn't as charming as usual, wasn't charming at all.

Sean did nothing because he didn't care if they had a tree or not—for him, this Christmas was to be his first *filets de caneton Tyrolienne*. Jim did nothing because during December he worked double time at the hospital. Hans did nothing because in his heart he knew that God would provide. His devotion to Christmas celebration was as sincere as it was sentimental; it just wouldn't be Christmas without a tree and lights and a nativity scene.

Days passed and trees were lit in all the front rooms of Oak Road and still the Thomasites had none. Finally Hans realized that unless he bought the tree himself, they would not have one. He dropped his memory book and hurried at once to Economart where he bought the largest tree they had.

The tree hadn't looked so tall in the parking lot, but in the house it took on new proportions. Hans and Billy wrestled with it for over an hour until, by cutting a foot off the bottom and a foot and a half off the top, they managed to make it stand in the living room. By this time it had no shape left at all; it was a huge green pillar that ran straight up and down. They hung a string of lights and a dozen red balls; they threw tinsel in thick lumps on the branches; then they stood back to admire their efforts. Even they could see that as a Christmas tree it wasn't much. Nor was their appreciation enhanced by Sean's remarking "Ah, the jolly green phallus" as he breezed through the living room.

Reginald was the only one who was pleased, getting up from his desk every hour or so and coming into the living room to refresh himself with a laugh at the tree. He loved it. It was a commentary on all the Thomasite decorations he had ever seen.

"You're becoming a cynic," Sean said.

"There's hope for me," Reginald said.

"There was a young cynic named Reg."

"You'll never rhyme it."

"At Christmas his teeth were on edge."

"Forced. You ought to be ashamed."

"It's true. I'm good only at the dirty ones."

"I'm going to your party, by the way." Reginald tried to sound casual, but he felt his neck begin to get red.

"Party?"

"The English party, at Dumpster House."

"Oh, that. I hadn't thought about going."

Reginald had thought about going. Indeed, in the past week he had thought of little else. He told himself he was looking forward to two things this Christmas: the English party was one and the other was the Midnight Mass he would celebrate at his family's dinner table.

And though he did not tell himself he was looking forward to the English party more than to the Mass, he knew it anyway and shrugged. You had to follow the Spirit.

16

Reginald stood in the Men's Room of Dumpster House, adjusting his tie before the mirror. I'm becoming a narcissist, he thought, because he had just said to his reflection, "You *do* look good."

Actually, Reginald had been the last one at the party to notice. Earlier in the week he had bought his first nonclerical suit, and along with it a small array of compatible shirts and ties. This evening, for the first time in his life, he had agonized over what tie would look best with his shirt, what socks would be most unobtrusive. He had even questioned whether a half-inch or more of shirt cuff should appear at his wrist.

The suit was a daring move for Reginald, but the shirt and tie even more so. Clerics at this time might occasionally wear brown shoes, they might even wear a tweed jacket and a polo shirt, but never, never, a tie. In some way no one had yet defined, a tie seemed to declare openly that the priest who wore it was edging out of the cloister and into the world. George had worn one for two years now and Bob Moran wore one, but he was a Jesuit. For Reginald the tie was a daring move indeed.

The door swung open and Reginald turned to see Malfoof Mihshay, miserable as ever.

"Happy Christmas, Malfoof!"

"I am dead by reason of the cold," he said sadly. "The fingers of my feet are frozen like to icicles." Shaking his head from side to side, he disappeared into the booth from which instantly there came a sound like a thunderclap.

Malfoof, like Reginald, was working for his doctorate in anthropology. No one knew anything about him except that he was a Lebanese of indeterminate age and inconsolable expression. He rarely spoke unless spoken to and, since his woeful looks did not encourage casual conversation, he was an unusually isolated figure on the University campus.

Reginald grinned into the mirror and began to comb his hair which was getting long and floppy. He had decided not to have it cut for a while.

The door swung open once again and George charged in looking distraught.

"Oh, there you are. I've been looking everywhere for you."

"Hi, old George. Happy Christmas!"

"Listen, Reg, I've got to talk to you for a minute. *You* know."

"Okay, sure. Why don't we go outside."

"No, this is good. This is better. I just want to get it over with quickly."

Reginald tilted his head toward the booth, but George did not notice. He was making the sign of the Cross.

"Bless me, Father, for I have sinned."

"No, George. Not here."

"Five times during the last week . . ."

His words were lost in another thunderclap from the booth, a long one ending in a high whistle. From behind the metal door, Malfoof sighed.

George went white, "Oh, God," he said and dashed from the Men's Room.

Reginald, relieved, returned to the party in Dumpster Lounge.

Dumpster House, a century old, had been designed for a clubby culture whose highest value was good manners and good breeding. This had given way in the near past to an academic culture which put a premium on intellectual competition. Most recently, there had sprung up a counterculture which leveled all differences of knowledge and breeding, a culture of homogenization. Through it all, Dumpster House had retained its integrity. The student suites stretched out in two long wings, but the center of the house—as the center of student lives—was the lounge. Nothing had changed that, not even the celebrated Bust of the previous spring.

The lounge was two stories high, rich with oak paneling

and huge vaulted windows. At the extreme end of the room, two entrances led to a double staircase that wound down to an elaborate parquet floor where leather chairs and sofas divided the room into conversational squares. Massive tables were littered with newspapers and magazines kept artfully disarranged.

This evening the leather furniture had been pushed against the wall and, in the center, the tables were covered with trays of Oreo cookies and crackers smeared with cream cheese and little brown things no one had yet identified. The English Department had at first agreed to sponsor the party but, after consulting its budget, had agreed to supply only the cookies and the glasses. In a panic over liquor, the student chairman had urged everyone to bring his own, which explained why no faculty members except the most desperately lonely had bothered to appear. Couples had arrived armed with brown paper bags, and now next to the cookies, stood a table sprouting bottles of odd sizes and shapes, most of them claiming to be scotch.

In its century of tradition, in its survival of clubby and academic and counter cultures, Dumpster House remained somehow removed from the abuses committed within its walls. It was above and apart from the shoddy buffets and the shabby scholars it maintained; the House, like God, was eternal and immutable and all good.

When Reginald returned to the lounge, he made straight for the liquor table. He was very nervous and he spilled the

Bobby Walker as he poured it into his glass. He examined the label on the bottle and then held his glass up to the light. He was surprised to see it was a plastic tumbler.

"Not exactly Waterford, is it." Sister Gunnekild appeared suddenly alongside the liquor table.

"Not exactly scotch either." Unconsciously he made his whimpering noise.

"Doris is here."

"Oh? That's good."

"Yes, Bob Moran invited us."

"Bob invited me too."

They stood looking around, with nothing to say to one another. It was still early in the evening, but already some drunk was carrying on loudly about the early Yeats. Hands were fluttering and there were protests of "No, no, the mature Yeats is the real Yeats," and they were all drinking very fast. Reginald and Sister Gunnekild moved away from the table.

"I see you've given up the habit too," Reginald said.

"It makes me feel more like a woman," she said.

"Ah." He wanted to say it was a pretty dress and she looked nice, but the fact was the dress was hideous and she looked terrible.

"Oh, look, there's Doris." She waved busily for Doris to join them.

"Hi, gang." It was the first Doris had seen of Reginald since his unkind rebuke. Uncertain what attitude she ought to adopt, she chose old chumminess, an attitude oddly out of place with her new hairdo and new gray silk cocktail dress. Beneath her chumminess lay sheer terror. As she approached Reginald, smiling broadly, he returned her smile and inwardly the terror vanished, leaving in its place a physical ache, a desire she had often felt for him but never before acknowledged. Bob Moran had been right.

She could not help herself. One hand crept forward and touched Reginald lightly on the chest. What on earth was she doing? The room spun for a moment and then she righted herself and said, "Lovely suit." She could not bear to look at him. "Bob Moran invited me," she said.

"Bob invited everybody," Reginald said.

"Ah, the sweet sound of my name." Bob made one of his unobtrusive entrances, on cue. They all said how glad they were to see him and, for differing reasons, they were.

"You must come over and laugh at our Christmas tree, Bob. It's a protest tree."

"When you've got a second, Reg." George signaled he would be waiting at the stairwell. He still looked distraught. Reginald wondered for a fleeting second who the lucky girl was this time.

"Thanks for inviting Malfoof," Doris said to Bob, "I think we've got him for the Lollipops."

"What's a protest tree?"

"Poor Malfoof, he's dead by reason of the cold."

"What does George want? He looks sinister skulking around like that?"

"Poor Malfoof."

"Well, at least he's black."

The noise in the room diminished suddenly and then receded altogether. There was one last cry of "the early Yeats" and the sound of laughter interrupted as everyone turned to look at the head of the double staircase. Natalie stood there, one hand resting lightly on the carved bannister, studying the little groups below. She wore a black lace dress and black stockings and her gleaming hair tumbled forward on her thin shoulders. She was oblivious to the silent staring. She stood there, completely in possession of herself and of the room. She gave a little wave and a smile of recognition as she saw the group she wanted. Slowly she descended the stairs and conversation began again, in low tones however, as if after some sacred act.

She walked straight to the group and said to Reginald, as if he were the only one there, "I hoped you would be here." Reginald could not answer, struck dumb with love.

After their meeting at Dumfey's, Reginald and Natalie had met everywhere on campus, always by accident, always with delight. Leaving the library one day, they met at the checkout desk and, since it was lunchtime, wandered together toward the Square. Reginald asked her to have lunch with him. As they were going into the Wursthaus Sean came by and asked if he might join them. The meal was spent in animated conversation between Sean and Natalie. Sean was writing a term paper on Crashaw as the first psychedelic poet and he went on and on about it, apologized for talking so much, and changed the subject to Melville about whom Natalie had theories no less unusual than his own. Reginald sat and marveled at how much he did not know. After that, he and Natalie had afternoon coffee together several times, and now it was Christmas and Reginald was splendid in his new green suit. And he was in love.

"I hoped you would be here," Natalie said, but Reginald could not answer. He stood there, smiling and smiling.

Doris was desolate in the Ladies' Room. She had had her hair cut straight and smooth, the sides slightly longer than the back and turned up at the front, a Streisand cut. She had bought a gray cocktail dress, very simple, very expensive; it would be her Christmas gift from Daddy. And she had spent an hour before the mirror examining her legs, her bust, the tiny lines beginning to appear beside her eyes and mouth.

She had realized the moment she saw Reginald why she had done all this. She was in love with him. A nun in love with a priest. It was sick, she told herself, it was disgusting.

She cried quietly for a while and then went back to the party, determined as a woman and a revolutionary not to show what she felt. She made straight for the liquor table where she met Malfoof Mihshay who was warming himself with scotch.

Reginald had finally remembered about George. He edged from one end of the lounge to the other and then back again, but was unable to find George anywhere. It was late in the evening by now and perhaps he had already left the party. Reginald felt a momentary twinge of guilt for having neglected to hear a man's confession.

George was a serious moral problem to Reginald anyway. As a priest, he could not refuse a man absolution when he confessed his sins, said he was truly contrite, and resolved to commit them no more. And yet there seemed little point in George's confessing in the first place since, whatever his sincerity might be, it never seemed to sustain him for more than a day at a time. Perhaps he would do better to leave the priesthood and perhaps it was a confessor's duty to say just that, or at least to suggest it. Reginald's suspicion was that he ought to see a psychiatrist; it could not possibly be normal for a man with a vow of chastity to be having sex with so many different girls. Could a confessor tell a man that what he needed was not a priest but a shrink? He would have to think about that.

And then he saw George. He was talking earnestly to a blonde girl several inches taller than himself. She made no effort to diminish her height. She had squared her shoulders and stood there, firm, sturdy as an Amazon.

What you see is what you get, Reginald said to himself, beginning to smile just as George turned and saw him.

George left the girl and went over to Reginald. "I've been thinking, Reg," he said, "this really isn't the place to go to confession. Why don't I stop by the house tomorrow. It's nothing pressing." And he returned to the girl.

That son of a bitch, Reginald said to himself, and set off to find Natalie who was dutifully making the rounds of her fellow graduate students.

"You've got to be passionate for freedom," Doris was saying, "you've got to be passionate for the rights of all peoples, especially the minority groups."

"Aiee, passion!" Malfoof said. This he could understand. No one in this mad country ever spoke of passion.

"Passion for freedom. Like for the blacks."

"I will not like the blacks; they are crazy Panthers."

"You have to understand the Panthers, Malfoof. They've been made what they are by a racist imperialistic culture. They're beautiful in their own way."

"I am Lebanese. I spit on Panthers."

"Lebanese? But I thought you were a black."

"Dusky," Malfoof said. "I am dusky and passionate." He filled her tumbler with scotch and then filled his own.

"Have you ever been in love?" she asked. Her eyes misted as she gazed through the black and sweating Malfoof and saw only the slick white form of Reginald, that ice-cream cone.

"Love," Malfoof whispered, "it is the only passion."

They had both had a great deal more drink than was wise.

"Men don't understand us, that's the whole thing," Sister Gunnekild said. She suspected Bob had said something upsetting to Doris and this was her way of telling him he should not have.

"Men understand, they just react differently," Bob said.

"They don't. How could they. Read Molly Bloom."

"Well, don't you think Joyce understood Molly Bloom?"

"The trouble is," Natalie said as she joined them, "men think we think. Women never think."

But before they could ask her to explain what she meant, she saw Reginald and went off to join him.

George was standing outside the Ladies' Room waiting for his Amazon when Doris and Malfoof approached him. They were wobbling noticeably.

"I've got to talk to you privately sometime, George," she said. "I need spiritual counsel."

"Yes, I can see," George said. He noticed her new dress. It was obviously expensive.

"I need spiritual advice," she said.

"Why don't you come by Winter Place and ask for me? I'm always home." Her hair had been cut, attractively too, he noticed.

"I need spiritual help," she said and went into the Ladies' Room, leaving George and Malfoof alone.

"I am Malfoof."

"Hello."

They shook hands, Malfoof grinning widely, George nervous and eager to get away.

"You are George."

"Right, George."

"Malfoof and George. I am Lebanese, George. I am not black. I spit on Panthers."

His tongue loosened by scotch and passion, Malfoof went

on chattering happily about Panthers and the Lebanese and Doris, "who weeps in the heart though the lips are smiling."

George merely stared at him, incredulous. As best he could make out, Malfoof actually believed he was not a black but a Lebanese. It was amazing what drink could do to a man.

At last the Amazon emerged from the Ladies' Room and George was able to spirit her away, his confidence somewhat shaken. There was nothing worse than a drunken black.

Everyone was leaving the party. There were groups at the telephone trying to get cabs and there were others at the door waiting for friends and there were people wrestling into coats and scarves and gloves, considerably hampered by drink and the crowded room and a common natural clumsiness.

Someone punched Reginald in the back as he helped Natalie on with her coat. He turned. The man apologized; he had been trying to get his fist through his sleeve. And then he looked at Natalie.

"Are you coming to the party?" he asked. "Come on to the party. You might as well."

Natalie and Reginald looked at one another questioningly.

"Let's," Reginald said.

"All right," she said. "It might be fun."

And so, packed into the back seat of a tiny green Volkswagen, they tore through the Cambridge streets in search of the party. The driver was very drunk, but the little car seemed to have an intelligence of its own and it darted the wrong way up one-way streets, dodging the oncoming cars and responding with little toots to the excited blasts of their horns. The couple up front, a thin economist and—on his lap—a Radcliffe secretary, applauded the driver as the car bounded into the Square and proceeded the right way up a one-way street. This struck them all as terribly funny.

Reginald's customary caution had long since disappeared and he was enjoying the crazy ride. He whimpered in Natalie's ear, explaining, "That's what the doggies do."

"That's sweet," she said. "Do it again."

"No, only once a day. Moderation in all things, St. Gommer says. Very important."

The driver suddenly made a number of quick left turns.

"We're lost." Natalie looked out the side window.

"That's nice," he said, gazing at her profile. He had almost decided to kiss her when the car lurched to a halt and they were there.

The party was on the second floor of what appeared from the outside to be an abandoned building.

"Who's the host?" Reginald asked Natalie as they climbed the narrow stairs.

"I don't know," she said. "Who's the fellow who drove us here?"

"I don't know. I thought he knew you."

"I thought he knew you."

But by then the door opened and someone shouted,

"Welcome to Green Street!"

Looking in, they could see that the floor was littered with cushions and bodies. Colored lights flashed startling patterns on the wall and the air was heavy with a Turkish scent. Acid rock blared in what was supposed to be the background.

"Come in, come," their host said. He was incredibly thin and wore neither shirt nor shoes. Around his neck hung innumerable strings of colored beads, a pair of white ducks clung at his hips. Somehow he conveyed the impression of being naked.

"Hello, darling," he said to Natalie and embraced her warmly. With Natalie still in his arms, he leaned across her and kissed Reginald. "You too, darling," he said, "so glad you could come. Now wait till I get you a little something for the trip."

It was that kind of party.

Reginald awoke the next morning sick. Somehow he had gotten home. Somehow he had gotten to bed. He lay there wishing he could die.

There was a strange taste in his mouth, not the kind of thing that came from drinking too much; this was like the taste of burned meat. Charred flesh. And then it came rushing back to him: the party on Green Street, the sweet sickening taste of the smoke, Natalie half-carrying him down the stairs to the Volkswagen.

Oh God, he thought, is this what comes of wearing ties?

17

Doris had found the five days following the English party difficult ones indeed. Sister Gunnekild and Bob Moran had taken her home despite, or because of, the protests of Malfoof who, in his gentle way, had begun to look forward to a night of Lebanese revels. She had slept soundly but when she awoke the next morning, the ceiling was still spinning and she could not make it stop. She padded to the bathroom and took a long drink of cold water. Immediately she began to wretch. "That's good, that's good," Sister Gunnekild said, pounding her on the back as if she had a fishbone stuck in her throat. After a long while there was no more to throw up and Doris sat back on her heels, resting her forehead on the cool rim of the toilet bowl. "I'm in love," she said and returned to her bed where she slept for several hours.

That evening and the next day she moped. She could not eat, she could not study. Sister Gunnekild suggested a film but Doris said no, not even "Casablanca." On the third day she broke down and, after a good hour's crying, told Gunnekild the truth; that she was in love with Reginald, who was so good and so beautiful and, oh God, it was awful, she couldn't help it, she was in love with him. They cried together for a while. A nun's life was a mystery and a sorrowful one.

By the fourth day, Doris had made a resolution. She

would see no more of Reginald. She would continue to attend the Lollipops, of course, and she would necessarily meet him at Sunday Mass at the old house on Winter Place, but there would be no more private conversations, no more walking him home, no more anything. She could see to that and she would.

Doris had been trained in the same school of moral theology as George St. George. A thing was good or bad, an action was right or wrong, there were no morally extenuating circumstances. In her own case the pattern of necessary action was clear. She was a nun in love with a priest. It was wrong to encourage this relationship in any way. Ergo, she must destroy this love, she must pluck it out root and branch. Didn't Christ Himself say, "Better to enter with one eye into the kingdom of heaven than with two to go to hell," or something along that line? Yes, she must do it, and so she would. Not for nothing had the simple doctrines of Christianity led her into revolutionary activities.

Such resolutions, she knew, are more easily made than kept. She would need encouragement, the tempered holy counsel of a priest. And so on the fifth day, the afternoon of Christmas Eve, she stopped in at Winter Place and asked Father Sheehey if she might have a word with Father St. George.

"I see, yes, I see," George said. "It must be very difficult as a religious of some—what is it, about ten?—years to suddenly find yourself in love. And have you, ah, done anything about this?"

"Well, yes, sort of."

"Sort of?" Sin is sin, he was thinking, there is no halfway mark. He knew.

"Yes, I've resolved not to see him alone, ever, and I'm going to do my best to pluck it out, root and branch."

Root and branch. Yes, they'd had the same training.

"But then again, I don't know. There's nothing really so wrong about being in love. I mean, do you think?" This was the kind of thinking she had not permitted herself when alone. With a priest you could say these things; since it was his job to restrain you, you could afford to let yourself go a little. "I mean, you can love someone without committing sin?"

"That's true, Sister. Dangerous, but true." George studied his hands, folded in his lap.

"You mean I'm kidding myself, don't you? I'm like a child who wants an ice-cream cone," she choked back a sob, "and will tell any lie to get it."

"Have you thought, Sister, that perhaps God might be calling you to his service in the lay state?"

She looked at him, shocked. Surely he was joking. But she could see he was not joking. She thought for a minute and then for another.

"I can't imagine not being a nun."

He remained silent, giving her imagination time to work.

"I mean, it just never crossed my mind."

"It was only a thought I had. Perhaps I shouldn't have said it."

"No, no. I'm glad you said it." She sounded heartbroken.

"Forget all about it. I should never have said it."

"No. That's okay, really, George. Father."

"Forget it."

They sat in the reception parlor, silent, each thinking of himself. There was no more to say.

"So thanks loads." She forced a smile. "You've been marv to listen to me."

She stood up and walked briskly to the door where she turned and gave him another smile, this one through tears. "See you," she said and stepped out into the cold, leaving George behind, filled with a mixture of satisfaction and compunction.

And so at Midnight Mass that evening Doris thought about the birth of Christ and her vocation and tried hard not to think about Reginald. And George, who was concelebrating the Mass with Father Sheehey and Bob Moran, thought with compunction about the ruins of his life and tried hard not to think about Doris who was looking very smart in a fitted winter coat and fur hat, further gifts from Daddy.

18

On December 31, 1969, almost everyone was making resolutions. They went like this:

Doris resolved to enter, open-minded, into the lay state. Her ten years as a Sister of Divine Prudence were over because she had discovered in herself certain worldly inclinations.

George resolved to give serious thought to his priesthood, but then again he always made that resolution whenever he was about to go to confession.

Natalie resolved to keep away from Reginald. Priests were trouble, even nice ones like Reginald.

Reginald resolved to give serious thought to his priesthood. He had considered resolving to keep away from Natalie, but decided that was too absolute a stand to take. He was against absolute stands and, besides, he had discovered in himself certain worldly inclinations which seemed all to the good.

Hans made forty-three resolutions which he recorded in his Light Book, a compendium of his spiritual insights. Of these resolutions he would keep only forty-two.

Michael McReedy shared his brother Francis' resolution to get the niggers that stomped them. He resolved also to fight back against his brother, or rather, as he put it to Francis himself, "to stop taking shit off you."

Sean and Billy and Jim made no resolutions at all and somehow their lives continued on much as if they had.

19

Sean stood in the kitchen shaking his Maxwell House jar while from the living room came the unaccustomed sound of female laughter. He would have liked to be there with them. Natalie was quick and had a good mind. And Barbie —God help us, *Barbie*—seemed less determined now that she was out from under the veil. He listened to the little trills of laughter. Jim had just told a gallows-humor story, in a cleaned-up version, about the emergency room at the hospital.

He gave another violent shake to his Maxwell House jar. He had heard the story before and it brought to mind a wonderful first line for a limerick, but he dismissed it as a distraction; good cooking demands complete attention. He held the jar up to the light. He was making salad dressing, a plain vinaigrette he would pour over the limestone lettuce leaves. He had discovered them that afternoon at the Foreign Food Mart in the Square and had provoked the clerk by giving him, in a thick German accent, a long dissertation on the peculiar merits of limestone lettuce. He smiled now as he thought of how annoying he had been.

The onion soup was simmering on the stove. The lettuce leaves were washed and ready to go. Petits pois smothered in butter. Rice verdi instead of potatoes. And his *escalopes de veau à la crème*. A simple meal, but one which required care. Sean was eager that it come out right, mostly because he was a perfectionist about his cooking, but also because he had played a large part in there being a dinner party in the first place.

Reginald had invited Natalie to dinner. Earlier in the week Reginald had told the others, over drinks, that they would be having a guest for dinner, a friend of his, not in anthropology, in English, uh, a girl actually, and so had ground to a halt. Hans went white, but said nothing. Sean was delighted to hear that the girl was Natalie Meyer. Billy, confused, kept asking why. And only Jim had had the sense to suggest Natalie might be more comfortable in a house full of men if another girl were invited as well. Hans choked on his Seven Up.

The only girl who came to Reginald's mind was Doris, and while he did not want to encourage her possessiveness and whatever fantasies might accompany it, he had to admit to himself that he had been unnecessarily distant recently. Still, he worried that a dinner invitation might more than make up for the injury, might even be construed as encouragement. And then, inspired, he thought of Gunnekild; he could invite them both and she would keep Doris in line and, more to the point, keep her off his neck. He now proposed inviting the three girls. Hans was adamant. One girl was bad enough but three was unthinkable, he said, and announced further that he would check with Father Provincial to see whether or not Canon Law forbade women entering the house of male religious.

An argument followed in which Reginald said very little, though Sean said many clever things and some unkind ones, making references as he rambled to Hitler and bunkers and the Thomasite Reich, all delivered in his provoking German accent. They ate in silence that night, without Hans, who had stormed off saying that if he got a phone call they could find him upstairs in his—he spat the word at Sean—bunker.

On the evening of the dinner Hans decided to eat out and, to everyone's relief, he did. To everyone's further relief, but especially Reginald's, Doris discovered she had a previous engagement, and so now Natalie and Sister Gunnekild—or Barbie, as she had begun to call herself—sat in the living room exchanging funny stories about car crashes they had been in.

Sean took the wine out of the refrigerator; it was a Pouilly-Fuissé '66, his favorite white burgundy. He held it to the light, pale gold, perfect. Now everything was ready to roll; the only problem was how to cook the veal without making everyone feel uncomfortable. There they'd be, three feet away, eating their soup. What they needed was a dining room. God, it was such a pain in the ass being poor sometimes. He listened at the living room door for a moment, wondering how to explain the situation.

"And then this car came smashing into the back of ours," Barbie said. "A police car, no less, and I was the only one without a seat-belt, so I went flying head-first into the windshield."

The flying nun, Sean said to himself, seeing her take off through the windshield, trailing a banner that said "I give a damn."

"Well, fantastic. I actually cracked the windshield. It

was *cracked!* Anyhow, we wore veils then that sort of locked around the head, so that none of your hair showed at all, and the windshield knocked my veil straight off, so the blood was running right down my face, really in a little trickle only, and my hair had just been cut, I kept it short, and it was sticking up in little lumps, sort of like miniature corn things, you know. And one of the policemen yanked the door open and saw me, this *nun,* you know, with no veil and cornstalks and blood, and he said to me, 'Oh my God, what do I do? What do I *do?*' "

The booze hath done her in, Sean said to himself.

"And I said to him, I said, 'I don't know, I've never done this before.' "

They all laughed and Sean smiled in spite of himself. He stepped into the living room.

"And if you think that's bad, what happened next was a man, he was bald with a velvet collar on his coat, and he pushed the policeman out of the way and he said to me, 'Don't worry, Sister, don't worry about a thing. I'm an undertaker.' An *under*taker!"

Barbie shrieked with laughter and then covered her mouth with both hands while the others laughed too and shifted in their seats. They all looked at Barbie curiously, never having seen her like this. And then Sean looked at Natalie who was looking at Reginald who was beautiful and dangerous. Jim only looked at his hands and reflected that there was a hell of a lot going on at the old duplex tonight.

Sean did not know how to begin. He was suddenly embarrassed, wished he were anywhere—even having dinner with Hitler—rather than here explaining that he would be cooking while they were eating. It was barbaric. It was a poor television comedy. And then his years of religious training came to his rescue and he assumed the stance that had allowed him to survive as a Thomasite—bravado.

" 'Sieurs, Dames. Old Father Gommer, ascetic that he was, would have us take our refection standing, staff in hand, ready to peel off when the fuzz should appear." He was proclaiming. "Since the Vatican Council, number two in the series, it has been the Thomasite custom to sit down for the principal meal. This is because we are modern members of a modern church. In this spirit, then, of a church on the move, would you kindly haul ass into the kitchen."

Barbie laughed, done in by drink.

"Oh, sorry," he said. In his enthusiasm for improvisation he had forgotten who was there.

Everyone agreed it was not fair that Sean should cook while they ate and so, with the soup cooling before them, they argued back and forth until Jim suggested they all eat now, together, and then just wait, wine in hand, while Sean played at being Escoffier.

And so Sean, giddy with nerves and delight, put on the crazy chef's hat they had given him at Christmas and performed.

" 'Sieurs, Dames," he began, and made a funny little bow. "You will observe that my scallops are of the palest pink and hammered to a thickness of one-quarter inch. One must always beat his scallops before cooking . . . oh, sorry. Voilà, the scallops. Now, into this lovely skillet and into that lovely skillet—we use two for greater speed—we place a little butter and about half as much cooking oil, and then we take a sip of our wine."

He moved with great speed and dispatch, his explanation timed perfectly to his gestures. His nervousness had disappeared. Cooking was his great joy. Cooking while showing off was a whole new experience and a heady one.

"Then, aha!, when the foam from the butter is just about kaput, we place on their tummies as many scallops as will fit, do you see—you, you, you, and you." Smoothly, expertly, he laid the scallops in the pan, his fingers skittering over the sizzling butter. "And so for this lovely skillet—you, you, you, and you. Never crowd the little buggers. Now, four, five minutes and you turn them over and roast their bums."

"I thought you all must be living on hamburger," Natalie said, "but Sean, you're so good. You really are."

"A mere nothing, my little chickadee," Sean said, becoming W. C. Fields for the moment and, in his excitement, putting his arms around her in a casual hug. The others pretended not to notice.

Natalie watched, fascinated, as he poured Madeira and beef bouillon into the skillets and boiled them along with the cooking juices, adding cream and arrowroot and herbs. She watched him slice mushrooms and sauté them. And she watched the final product emerge, the perfect beautiful platter with scallops in the center and heaped around them

21

Why was it, Natalie wondered, that the only men she found attractive were Thomasite priests. Despite her contention that women do not think, Natalie had thought about this question all during January and now, on St. Valentine's day, waiting for Reginald to arrive at her apartment, she was thinking about it still.

George had been a mistake, there was no doubt about that, but how could she be sure Reginald was not equally a mistake? Did she love him or was it just some strange kind of fascination, his beautiful face, perhaps, or the promised perfection of his body beneath those light clothes he wore?

Natalie had given a great deal of thought to Reginald's face. Some weeks earlier, in fact, before he had begun to grow the beard, she had sketched him during a seminar they were taking—Reginald had gone to the trouble of cross-registering in both anthropology and English this semester. While an enthusiastic graduate student with bulging eyes had lectured endlessly about phallic symbolism in *Women in Love*, his eyes blinking, bulging even larger whenever he mentioned Gudrun, Natalie tilted her chair back from the table and drew several Reginalds in profile until he suddenly shifted in his chair and she was able to capture him full face. At the end of the session she put her notes aside and did not think of the sketches again until the following week on her way to the seminar, when they fell from her notebook. She examined them curiously, from a merely technical point of view, checking the definition of line and the sharpness of resemblance. She was astounded to see that the face she had drawn was very nearly her own, not because like most amateur draftsmen her portraits of other people always resembled herself, but because in fact she and Reginald looked enough alike to be twins. They had the same huge brown eyes, heavy-lashed and warm, and their cheek and jaw structures were the same. The resemblance was extraordinary.

Was that the fascination, she wondered. Narcissism? A kind of incest. Or at any rate, incest without the taboo. She thought of Byron with his wild curls and burning eyes; on the whole she preferred Reginald. But when she saw him at the seminar that day sporting a three-day growth of beard, she was relieved.

"Do you think it's dumb?" he asked.

"I think it's sweet," she said.

Their mouths were different, she observed, Reginald's being wide with slightly heavy lips that were maddeningly sensuous. Not like her own at all.

"I think it will look just perfect," Natalie said, pleased they would not now look so much alike.

But her pleasure did not last. It was succeeded almost immediately by a feeling of annoyance that men become priests in the first place. Why did they do that? It was unnatural. It was . . . what?

She wished there were someone she could ask about it. Sean came to mind, but that was ridiculous; he was still a boy. Sister Gunnekild came to mind, making Natalie shiver. Gunnekild–Barbie–she was convinced, was a dangerous woman.

Three or four times since Reginald's dinner, Barbie had swooped down on her with intimate and unsettling questions. "Are you Jewish?" "Do you think Reginald understands you, as a woman, I mean?" "What do you mean when you say women don't think?" In regard to this last, Barbie had quoted at great length a three-way conversation that had taken place at the English Christmas party. Listening to her, Natalie thought, this is a dangerous woman, and decided she did not like Sisters at all. No, Barbie was not the one to ask about priests. Nor Bob Moran either, the Eyes and Ears of the World.

Still, it was Bob Moran who shortly afterward forced on her a copy of *Picnic in Babylon*, a diary by one of his Jesuit friends. The jacket promised something about the inside story of a priestly vocation and Natalie went at the book with the enthusiasm she had once brought to Middle English. That enthusiasm dwindled, however, as she recognized on page after page the infallible pronouncements of a closed mind. This man was so sure, so positive, but how did he get that way? And why? The book, pious and determined, offered no clue.

The author had read widely, however, and it was his comments on modern literature that proved valuable to Natalie, not in themselves but in what she was able to conclude from them about the way Catholics think. The peculiar logic that had so often organized the rant of George St. George had always amused her. But now she discovered that this same logic was in a subtle way what determined Reginald's many measured silences. Catholic logic, she called it, this peculiar habit of insisting upon a single central point, whether the subject of discussion was D. H. Lawrence or Sacred Scripture.

The process of reaching that single central point operated in two distinct ways. In George, it was a matter of cutting away all irrelevant side issues; anything that led the judicial mind from the central point rather than to it was discarded. In Reginald she had observed a more patient, perhaps more priestly, method; Reginald pursued an argument in decreasing concentric circles. He spoke discursively, handling side issues as he progressed, never sidestepping a knotty question, until at last there was no point at issue except the central one. George was linear, Reginald was cyclic, but both were experts in Catholic logic. And what made it Catholic was that for George and Reginald, and perhaps for all Catholics, every issue—whether political or literary or social—resolved finally into a moral or theological premise. It was a way of Catholicizing all reality.

Sometimes in class she would listen to Reginald speak, smiling to herself as she predicted what, according to Catholic logic, he would say next. Usually she was right, but she remained troubled by whatever it was that lay beneath the biased logic—a conviction of some sort, a powerful one. She determined to get at it.

Since his dinner party Reginald had phoned at least once a week to ask if he could see her. And he would arrive, beaming and only a little awkward, clutching his bottle of wine. They would talk about books and the tedium of the University; they would talk about their present lives, but little about their pasts, and only rarely about their childhoods, Reginald's being dull and Natalie's being mysterious. Whenever conversation threatened to turn from the personal to the romantic, they would listen to music. Theirs was still an undeclared love affair.

Now and then she had startled him with unlikely questions.

"What are the seven capital sins?"

Reginald thought a moment, first of Natalie—a fascinating mind, you sometimes forgot she was a girl at all—and then of the sins.

"I'm not sure I remember," he said. "Let's see. Pride, covetousness, gluttony, anger, envy, sloth. How many is that? Oh, and lust."

He grinned, thinking of Natalie again.

And once she had asked him why the Pope felt he was infallible when it was so evident that a human mind could grasp any problem only humanly and that obviously left room for error. Reginald agreed with her.

"But what happens to Infallibility then?"

"It stays on the books, I guess. What does it matter?"

Catholic logic, she decided, was more complex than at first appeared.

As for Reginald, he was as pleased to talk with her about the failings of his Church as about the failings of the University. He was in love and being with her was the only thing that mattered. Not that he would ever tell her he loved her—he knew that would complicate the friendship and perhaps even end it—but love was good, he told himself, and women were good and the beautiful Natalie was the best of all.

Feeling as they did, they were equally unprepared for what happened that night on the fourteenth of February after Reginald knocked on the door and, struck once more by Natalie's slender beauty, said to her, "I love you."

While Natalie had spent much of her day pondering the peculiar attraction of Thomasite priests and wishing it were not so, Reginald had kept his New Year's resolve by giving serious thought to the question of his priesthood.

Reginald had kept his resolution more by accident than by design. First there had been the incident with George, who on the first day of 1970 showed up at Reginald's room saying he wanted to start the new year with a general confession. Both of them were suffering from hangovers, Reginald's less acute and without the added sting of guilt that disturbed George, and so both were particularly open to the operations of the Holy Spirit, or so they felt. George intoned his list of sins with a solemnity he thought proper to a general confession. Like most Catholics, the only sins he considered worth bothering about were sexual, and so he began with his only real affair—Natalie of course remained nameless—and went on to a truly dizzying series of seductions, betrayals, fornications, and adulteries. Reginald had heard only random confessions from George and was not prepared for this general summation. Where *were* all these girls, he found himself thinking, and why wasn't George worn out? More to the point, why didn't George *get* out? "You seem to be in training for some sort of sexual Olympics," he said, and having committed himself to a firm line, told George further that what he needed was not a confessor but a psychiatrist. George was indignant and demanded his absolution, got it, and left. Two weeks later he began consulting one of the several University psychiatrists, but he refused Reginald the satisfaction of telling him so. Reginald was convinced he had said what he should have, but afterward whenever he saw George—who seemed these days to be always trailing Doris about the campus—he thought of his own priesthood and his real and growing love for Natalie.

Then there was Bob Moran who was pushing *Picnic in Babylon* to all his friends. The book eventually reached Reginald and disturbed him profoundly because he kept identifying with the author. There were similarities which explained this: their ages were the same, their religious training similar, they were both enthusiasts. Furthermore, their motivation for becoming priests was identical. And this was what disturbed Reginald most, for from the tone of the book he was certain of one thing: the author was an introverted, unhappy young man who ought never to have been a priest. And what about me, he wondered.

And then most recently, that very afternoon in fact, he had finished reading *To the Lighthouse* and, putting the book down, said aloud to himself, "I'm alone. And I don't want to live alone." He sat for a while looking into the empty street and then went upstairs to talk to Sean who was in a terrible depression himself. Sean, however, had the gift of being able to put aside depression as if it were an uninteresting newspaper and he did so now, amusing Reginald with an hour or more of University anecdotes, most of which he made up himself, and when Reginald left his room, Sean picked up his depression where he had left off. Reginald went to the shower where he soaped himself vigorously and sang off key, his good spirits restored. But drying himself, he became conscious of his hands moving on his flesh as if they were the hands of someone else. Natalie, he thought, and immediately, I don't want to live alone.

He phoned Natalie and asked, as he often did, if he might come over and visit. He was in love with her—not that he would ever tell her that—and love was good, and women, and Natalie was best of all. Because of that, because he must not risk their friendship for the sake of indulging a momentary feeling, he must not talk to her about love.

Feeling as they did, then, they were equally unprepared for what happened that night when Reginald stood at Natalie's door, wine in hand, and was struck once more by her desirable beauty.

"I love you," he said, staring, shaking a little.

"What a sweet thing to say," she said, with a small, nervous laugh. "Come in, come in, you'll catch your death just standing there in the door. Here, give me your coat.

Oh, that lovely scarf, that's my favorite scarf. Why don't you put your coat on the daybed and I'll go and . . ." Her voice trailed off into the kitchen. She was determined she would not get involved with him until she was certain she loved him. But in the kitchen, rattling through the knives in search of the corkscrew, she asked herself how you could be in love without being involved first. Priests are dangerous, she reminded herself, and at that moment cut her finger on a paring knife. It was a tiny cut, but it gave her the opportunity of introducing a distraction when she returned to Reginald who stood grinning in the other room.

Later, when they had drunk half the wine and were sitting together on the daybed, Natalie asked one of her startling questions.

"Tell me about priests," she said. "Why do men become priests?"

Reginald gave her a long answer, a masterpiece of Catholic logic, she thought, and went on to the story of his own vocation which seemed to bear no resemblance to the normal way men decide to become priests. He touched on the difficulties of the life, not the obvious ones like the vows or celibacy, but the hidden ones like loneliness, the awful awareness that life must be lived totally alone.

"What about God?" she said.

"What about Him?"

"Well, I thought He was supposed to make up for all that. Like the way nuns are supposed to be the brides of Christ? Don't they say that? I remember my mother once saying that. It sounds like an invention of Poe."

They went off on a discussion of Poe.

Later still, when they had nearly finished the wine, Reginald asked how her mother knew about brides of Christ and Natalie told him about her mother, a Jew who had spent seven years of her life concealed in a convent of Belgian nuns, had married an American textile importer immediately after the war, and who now, at forty, was divorced and beautiful and a complete stranger in a Kibbutz in Israel.

Reginald put his arm around her, having no words to cope with melodrama. Natalie laid her head on his shoulder.

When the wine was done, Reginald got up from the daybed and moved to a chair where he sat, elbows on knees, chin in hands, thinking. Natalie remained on the daybed, trying not to think.

After a long while Reginald looked up and smiled at her.

"I love you."

"I know," she said.

"I want to make love to you."

Natalie said nothing.

"I want to go to bed with you."

Still she said nothing.

"Does that offend you? I didn't mean to offend you."

"No. No, that isn't it at all. I'd like to sleep with you too, but I can't. It will just, you know, complicate your life too much."

"It's already pretty complicated."

23

"I'm becoming a narcissist," Doris said to herself. She turned slowly before the full-length mirror, keeping a watchful eye on how her behind looked in the new pants suit. "And high time, too," she added.

She had wanted a pants suit to wear while entertaining George, but now that she had it, she was doubtful. Protection of some kind was necessary, yes, but protection that made your behind stick out? And her walk was too manly anyhow. The little homosexual at T. Jones had told her she looked heavenly in it, and it was true that in the shop her behind had seemed smaller, but home in the harsh light of her bedroom, all the behind had reappeared.

"No," she said, "not even for protection."

George was coming over for a drink this evening. He would have been over every evening if she let him, but there were some times she liked to be with Malfoof and occasionally she liked to be alone. Malfoof always took her out to Lebanese restaurants while George, being a priest, would bring his wine and sit for the evening listening to her stereo.

George had been the first guest in her apartment, arriving in fact even before the furniture. He had been impressed by the apartment, a five-room affair on Brattle Street, and was more impressed by the furniture when it came, Danish modern that was so expensive it looked good. Daddy had insisted, Doris explained.

Daddy had insisted because there was nothing too good

for his Doris. Ellsworth Hanlon, owner of Hanlon Fuel, was a man of unlimited generosity and of nearly unlimited means. He had hoped for a large family but resigned himself easily to being the father of a single daughter, his resignation turning to a sort of tragic acceptance when Doris entered the Sisters of Divine Prudence. And so her announcement that she was leaving the convent spurred him to furious acts of buying; it was he who chose the apartment and he, his ghastly taste relieved only slightly by the palliative of money, who chose the Danish modern and managed to have it delivered in an impossible two weeks. And why not, he liked to say, wasn't she the unprodigal daughter back in the world at last?

Following Daddy's lead, Doris threw her considerable energies into becoming a woman rather than an ex-nun. She had made a beginning with the beauty parlor and the cocktail dress; she now made daily forays into the boutiques on Newbury Street, buying cashmere sweaters at Antell, alligator shoes at Papagallo, and dresses everywhere and in every color except black. She bought expensive art books, records, a stereo; she bought two paintings and a bit of sculpture. She fitted out a little marble-topped table as a bar. Furthermore, she did all this oblivious to the expense involved. Her only prick of conscience came when she considered that these things were for herself.

And so this evening, turning before the mirror to check her behind in the new pants suit, she remarked to herself, "I'm becoming a narcissist," and then recalling all those years of not being even a person, let alone a narcissist, she added, "and high time, too." She removed the pants suit and put it away forever in her ample closet. She would simply have to face George tonight without protection.

Doris herself knew she exaggerated the need for protection, since George was harmless enough if you kept him at a distance, and besides she enjoyed being treated like a woman. She also enjoyed the game they were playing, she insisting that her only passions were of the mind and spirit, George doing his best to introduce her to the passions of the flesh.

"But just let me, just let me," he would say, exasperated, as she pushed away the hand he had spent an hour easing inch by inch from her shoulder to her breast.

"You're supposed to be a priest," she would say.

"Priests are human," he would say.

And indeed, to George's mind, prodded on as it was by the University psychiatrist, priests seemed daily more and more human.

"You're a man," he told George, "every man needs a good fuck. The trouble with you is you feel guilty about it." The University allotted only eight hours of psychiatric help to any given student and George's doctor took pride in the fact that none of his patients had ever required more than six. "You've got to stop feeling guilty," he told George, "priests are only human."

So it was with an increasingly lighter conscience that George pursued girls to their beds, though he was still a little uncomfortable saying Mass the following day. He had given up confession altogether. "Priests are human, after all."

With time, of course, he had worn down some of Doris' resistance—nothing inflamed him quite so much as a girl's indifference to him—and he was sure the rest would follow any day. His abiding fear was that Malfoof would get there first.

His fears were justified since Malfoof's pursuit of Doris was aided by the many natural advantages he enjoyed. Not only was he black, he was alone and miserable as well. Further, he was gentle, almost courtly in his attention to Doris. And finally, there was his appreciation of passion. It is all one, he insisted, none of this mind and spirit and flesh; the flesh *is* the spirit. Doris did not understand that, but she liked the sound of it. "Silly Binky, you are," she would say to him, and he would writhe in his chair, monstrously erect.

With Malfoof, she thought, she needed protection from herself.

George looked around appreciatively. He liked this apartment, it had style, it had class. And especially, it had money. Good taste always made him feel sexy.

"Tonight's the night," he said, handing Doris the wine.

"George, you're the awfullest priest," she said and went to the kitchen for a corkscrew.

George busied himself with the stereo. He piled up "Let

It Be," "Bridge Over Troubled Waters," and on top of them four Vivaldis, music timed to the progress of the evening. He had had the unhappy experience of trying to make love with Streisand belting out "Happy Days Are Here Again" in the background. Now, whenever possible, he chose the evening's music himself.

"I feel good tonight." He took the corkscrew from Doris.

"You look good tonight," she said.

George gave her a knowing glance and a knowing laugh.

She liked the game they were playing.

Later, when the wine bottle was half empty, Doris suddenly asked him, "Why are you a priest? I mean, why do you stay one?"

They were lying on the floor, Doris rubbing one bare foot on the thick crimson shag rug, George tracing the outline of her breast where he had finally managed to get his hand.

"You really don't seem much the priest type." For the moment she had decided to let his hand stay where it was.

"Maybe I'll leave. I don't like to talk about it."

"Don't leave," she said. She liked the feel of his hand on her breast.

"I meant the priesthood."

"Oh, that."

He grasped the breast more firmly in his hand, ran his thumb over the nipple, as best he could, given that damned brassiere.

"Are you just waiting to get your degree?"

around him and he had gone rigid all over for a minute and then said, "Oh Christ," and just flopped over on his side. That must have been what he meant by drowning. "I don't know," she said, "it's more like sit-ups or something, like when you do the Canadian Air Force Exercises."

George rolled over on his side to stare at her in disbelief. The Canadian Air Force Exercises?

"God, don't shake that sheet," she said. "It's like Revere Beach down there. Low tide." She began to giggle.

George had never known anyone so crude. There was no denying, though, she certainly brought enthusiasm to sex.

"Let me look at your little thing again," she said.

George was not sure how much more of this he could endure.

Doris was surprised the next morning to feel no sense of guilt whatsoever. She felt a bit sore physically and she had bruises on the inside of her hips—George had risen to the occasion twice more during the night—but spiritually she felt marvelous. She wondered why this was so.

Her mind drifted back to her early years in the convent. She had always been the first in chapel for morning visit, the last to leave after evening prayers. She had always volunteered for the unpleasant jobs, cleaning the toilets, nursing the old Sisters. The floors she waxed had gleamed more golden than any others. And when she was assigned to teach grammar school, her classes were the brightest and—more important—the best behaved. And now here she was sexing it up with a priest. Enjoying it!

How strange I am, she thought. But not really *so* strange if you look at it as a channeling of energies. There's no point in doing something unless you put your whole self into it. Sex included.

She began to hum "All, or nothing at all."

Sex. Really, thinking about it, there was nothing much wrong with it. There was nothing at *all* wrong with it. It was like Canadian Air Force Exercises, invigorating, and you'd scarcely feel guilty for exercising. She would see how she felt about it later in the day.

She rolled over in bed and giggled, thinking of George's little thing. It was adorable.

"I've come a long way from the convent," she said aloud, adding, "and high time, too."

The phone rang and it was George—who had left only four hours ago—asking if he might come over. She told him to phone back in the evening when she would know how she felt about it. A few hours later the phone rang again.

"Just let me come over," he said, "Just for an hour." It was midafternoon, but he had been unable to hold out until evening.

"No, George," she said, "not for a while."

"I just want to talk. I won't do anything, I swear it."

"Not for a while, George. 'Once makes you a philosopher, more than once makes you a sodomist.' Voltaire said that in a different context, but you see what I mean."

"I'll phone tonight," he said.

He presumed that she was suffering the pangs of guilt he had experienced at the beginning of his own sexual career, but he was mistaken. Doris was precipitate in all things, but she invariably acted on principle and she had not yet had time to formulate a principle on sex. Later in the week, following a night spent with the courtly Malfoof, she would do so. At the moment, however, six weeks out of the convent and six hours out of bed, Doris was between principles.

They had been to dinner at the Athens Olympia to celebrate St. Valentine's day. Throughout the meal Doris had spiced her conversation with references to Steve McQueen's extraordinary attraction, and then to Dustin Hoffman, a more sensitive actor, and finally to Sidney Poitier, whom she found irresistibly sexy. Malfoof uncrossed his legs and crossed them again. She gave him longing looks and he fidgeted in his seat. She called him Binky and during dessert, while he devoured her with his sad and passionate eyes, she did not look away but let herself be eaten.

Doris had not seen George in several days though he had continued to phone and to trail after her across the campus. After much thought, she had decided she was not in a position to formulate a principle on sex, her experience being limited and perhaps inadequate. Malfoof came to mind as another possible source of experience; poor Malfoof, such a lovable, sad Binky. If Malfoof persisted, she thought, then she would let him. And in truth, by the time they reached the Athens Olympia, she was doing all she could to make him persist, nor did she slacken her efforts when they returned to her apartment.

"Have a little drink, Malfoof, for Valentine's day. I

bought some Arak because I thought you might like it."

"Arak," he said, "the tears of the Prophet." He held the clear liquid up to the light. "Ayni," he said, "ayouni."

"Silly Binky," she said.

Later, lying on the thick crimson shag rug with Vivaldi playing in the background, Doris said, "Tell me about passion, Malfoof, I don't understand about passion."

"Aiee, passion!" he said and explained to her, with references to Al Ghazali and the Koran and the Canticle of Canticles, that the flesh *is* the spirit, that all passion is one. The explanation remained rather more academic than Doris had hoped and so she laid her head on his chest–she was trying to remember how it had happened with George–and placed her hand on his stomach, her little finger tucked inside his belt.

"My nice Binky," she said and moved her hand slowly across his stomach. Immediately his trousers began to bulge along his left leg, his stomach tightened, his breathing stopped. She looked up at him, alarmed. "Are you all right?" she said.

"It is the passion," he said, his teeth gritted. "Ayni," he said, "ayouni. I am trying to resist."

"I thought you were having an attack," she said.

"It is the passion."

"Do you want to come to bed with me?"

He only stared at her, astounded.

"Come to bed with me."

Doris lay in her huge Hollywood bed listening to the

shower run in the bathroom. Malfoof was preparing. What preparations were there, she wondered, and was *she* supposed to be preparing too? Perhaps she should have asked him. But he had simply risen from the floor, kissed her gently on the left eye then on the right, and saying, "I am making my preparations," he had disappeared into the shower. So unlike George, she thought. The shower had stopped now and she could hear Malfoof applying the towel with great vigor. She wondered whether he would dress again or come into the room naked. She herself had put on a filmy white nightgown that emphasized her waist and minimized her behind, or so she thought.

And suddenly there he was, his black body naked and startling against the white walls and the white carpet.

"This is me," he said, stretching his arms straight out from his shoulders, offering himself.

Doris was not prepared for what she saw. Malfoof clothed was a melancholy little man, but Malfoof naked was an ebony statue of elegant proportion. His face no longer looked gray and morose; it was black and gleaming, framed in ringlets of wet hair. He had a short thick neck that ran into shoulders more heavily muscled than she would have thought, and his arms, extended toward her, were long and graceful. His chest was heavy and tapered to a waist Doris herself might have envied. But then her gaze stopped. It must be her eyes, she thought. She looked away, thinking of George, and then looked back again quickly. It was true.

"Your thing," she said. "My God, look at the size of your thing!"

"This is so," he said, and came toward her, lobbling. "The length, it is of the stallion. The strength, it is of the ram's horn. But the length and the strength are not what matters. What matters is the quality of the performance."

Afterward, she understood what he meant.

24

Cunning and chance had aided Michael and Francis McReedy in their plans for revenge against the Panthers.

Grandma Shea's chemistry set had proved valuable not so much for what it accomplished but for the possibilities it suggested. Shortly after the new year Francis stole from the chemistry closet at school a large selection of small bottles labeled "dangerous." By experimentation, but mostly by accident, he discovered that dilute hydrochloric acid mixed with sulfuric acid causes an explosion both frightening and deadly.

He had poured a small amount of something into a test tube and from the little line of bottles he chose the nearest;

before he could add anything else the mixture began to smoke and then to rise rapidly in the glass tube. The two boys bent closer and, suddenly realizing it might explode, Francis turned the mouth of the tube away from his face. As a consequence the foaming acid caught Michael in the side of the neck and ran down his sweater. Michael fled screaming upstairs while Francis, in the interest of science, examined the two bottles and set them carefully aside: hydrochloric acid, sulfuric acid. Michael's neck was burned, though not badly, and his sweater was ruined; the boys were forbidden ever again to play with the chemistry set. As for Grandma Shea, she was punished with a special silence, no one even making the effort to speak to her, and Francis called her "fat ass" three times and got away with it.

A week later the local police made a raid on Weatherman headquarters, or what they thought were headquarters, and came away with two copies of *The Revolutionary's Handbook*. As it happened, Weatherman was located in the apartment next door and the captured books belonged to an undergraduate and his girlfriend and were the assigned texts for a Social Questions seminar they were taking at the University. This in no way fazed Officer McReedy who, though he had not been in on the raid, brought one of the books home and slapped it on the kitchen table as evidence that he was doing all he could to make up for the stomping of his sons.

Francis leafed through the book—there was an awful lot about organizing crowds and the proper conduct of a riot—until he came to the section, "Notes on a Private Arsenal."

Molotov cocktails, grenades, napalm: it was a "how-to" section, exactly what he had been hoping for.

He took it the next day to Kopy King, a former shoeshine parlor that now specialized in pornography, marijuana, off-track gambling, and document reproduction.

"It's illegal to xerox that stuff," the girl said. She was mammoth and chocolate brown. Francis noticed even through her heavy sweatshirt that she was not wearing a brassiere.

"It's illegal to run a numbers racket," he said.

"I don't mess with that stuff," she said, pointing at the *Handbook* open before her.

"It's illegal to push grass," he said.

"What's your name, anyhow, you little mothah?"

"Fucky," he said.

"I believe it," she said.

Nonetheless she xeroxed the pages for him.

"Here you go, muhfuh."

"Buy a bra," he said.

For the next several weeks Michael and Francis worked furiously with old Alka Seltzer bottles and wads of cotton and gasoline. Frequently they came up with something that looked right and that had been built according to rigid specifications, but nothing ever worked. Michael lost interest and began constructing a crane with his erector set. Francis was not discouraged, however, and it was his perseverance that finally put into their hands a creditable molotov cocktail which, when they hurled it late one night against the school handball courts, burst magnificently into flame and took a good-sized chunk of concrete from the wall. Now that he had the formula, Francis made a cocktail whenever he could get his hands on an Alka Seltzer bottle, most of which he found in the Thomasite rubbish, Alka Seltzer being Sean's specific against hangover. Francis stored these in the Thomasite cellar under a heap of rags, far away from the prying eyes of his mother. Michael once again joined him in their project.

It was cunning and chance together which enabled them to get hold of the dynamite. The University had recently decided that it was now safe to level the wreckage of the burned house which had been the object of last fall's protest rally; excavations were at last in progress for construction of the ten-story drama center. The building company had run into bedrock and had hired the Acme Powder Blasting Corporation to complete the work of excavation. Francis watched for his chance and during the actual moment of a blast, when everyone including the guard was absorbed in work at the site, he climbed into the rear of the truck and stole the dynamite. It was dark inside and there were heaps of wire and coils of things he couldn't make out, but at once he spotted the Danger sign on a steel box, its cover open, and large gray sausages lying in it side by side. He was surprised at how heavy they were. He had four or five cradled in his arm when suddenly the guard behind him bellowed and Francis, with great dexterity, shoved one inside his belt and made a show of putting the others back. Despite this, the guard made an effort to grab him, but Francis punched him in the belly and ran down Irving Street and across winter Place, zigzagging his way home. In the Thomasite cellar he examined his useless stick of dynamite. He hadn't expected a wick, of course, but he realized from *The Revolutionary's Handbook* that without a detonator cap the stick was useless. Just the same, it was a handy thing to have; you could never tell what you might use it for some day. He placed it under the pile of rags with the molotov cocktails.

That night he told fat Judy Molocha he had something to show her. After she had seen the stick of dynamite he showed her other things which pleased her even more because she was fat and today was St. Valentine's day.

25

"There was an old card shark out west
Whose genitals grew from his chest.
This hindered romance
But gave him the chance
To play his cards close to the vest."

Sean printed the limerick carefully on a three-by-five filing card and placed it in his recipe box behind the little blue tab marked "personal." Because his handwriting was nearly illegible even to himself and because sometimes his hand shook so much he could not control a pen, Sean usually relied on the typewriter. Today, however, St. Valentine's day, he was in a deep depression and could not muster the energy that somehow went with the idea of controlling a machine. So he sat at his desk printing.

> "Of that amorous señor from Chile
> All the sweet señoritas asked, 'Will he
> Simply knock on the door
> Like a gentleman, or
> Pick the lock with his membrum virile?' "

He finished printing and read over what he nad composed. A bit tortured maybe? Well, you try rhyming Chile, he thought, and plopped the card into "personal." Something to show his grandchildren when they ask if priests ever get bored. He took another card.

> "A champion crapper named Flushmore
> Said that he never would blush more . . ."

What's the use, he thought, what am I doing here? Lately, ever since Reginald's dinner for Natalie and that one, that Barbie, he had been uneasy, not with the usual frustration of wanting to be a poet and not being able to, but with a sense of not belonging, of something missing both in himself and in his life. It couldn't be sex, he told himself, because he didn't know anything about sex, didn't care about it. He thought of Natalie standing next to the stove, impressed with his cooking. But it wasn't that, it went deeper than that. If he were like Reg, for instance....

As if summoned, Reginald came into his room. And Sean, putting aside his own depression, charmed Reginald out of his gloom with bizarre stories about University goings-on, most of which he made up himself. After an hour or so Reginald went off, whistling, to the shower and Sean said to himself, poor Reg, he's in love.

Later, as he prepared dinner, he was in one of his remote moods, so the others stayed out of his way. Hans and Billy argued while Reginald and Jim stood by.

"No, no," Hans said. "A man who exposes himself to only one point of view can never be a historian—he is merely the member of a fashionable political cult."

That stopped Billy dead, and indeed the others as well.

Sean glanced at Reginald to see how he was taking the wit and wisdom of Hans Berger and was astonished at the look on his face. Was he sneering? Reginald was becoming a very different man. Annoyed, he returned to the stove where he was putting last touches on an aromatic coq au vin. He rattled several pots, only half listening to the conversation, until suddenly he heard Hans say, "Hitler wasn't *all* bad, you know. The Jewish problem has been much exaggerated."

"Oh, for Christ's sake, Berger, you make me sick," Sean said. "The only time you're broadminded is when it's a question of burning Jews." Oh God, he thought, I'm shaking hell out of the coq au vin.

"Now, Sean, now, Sean," Hans said.

There was suddenly a whoop as Francis McReedy, trailed

by Michael, cleared the fence in the back yard and went clattering down the outside stairs to the cellar. A door slammed shut.

"Besides," Sean shouted, "you should never have told those little bastards they could play in our cellar; they're going to blow up the goddam house one of these days."

"Now, Sean, now, Sean," Hans said again.

"Oh, go . . ." he couldn't think of anything appropriate ". . . go masturbate," he muttered, and turned off the gas beneath the coq au vin.

Much later that evening, very near midnight, Sean was thinking of his life in the protest community. What was he protesting, except the religious life itself? And Reg? What was happening to him? Billy, non-existent. Jim, who knew Jim? And as for Hans—there was a noise from the room upstairs, Hans' room, the only one on the third floor—probably whacking off, Sean thought, and said aloud, "God, forgive me," and then thought to himself, but it's probably true. Anybody that righteous . . . oh, forget it.

He thought of himself, drinking. He had entered the Thomasites because that seemed a good way of serving God and being a teacher. But if what went on at the University was teaching, he didn't much want that, and as for God, well, there was service and service. To cook or consecrate, he thought, and poured another scotch.

"Happy Valentine's day all around," he said, toasting imaginary lovers wherever they might be and several real ones whom he knew quite well. To cook or consecrate, that is the question.

26

St. Gommer, around the turn of his century, began to find the long weeks from February to April more trying than in his youth. He was afflicted by long bouts of depression and during one of these he had wondered aloud if the Thomasite Order—our littlest Order, he called it—was all it ought to be. He took his doubts and his depression to his confessor, a man blessed with small intellect but great common sense, who assured Gommer that his Order would never be all it ought to be and he would do well to face that fact and live with it. And live with it cheerfully, the confessor added, himself famed for conviviality.

St. Gommer had thereupon prescribed for February and March a litany of celebrations both sacred and solemn with much pomp and, insofar as Lent would admit, a bit of feasting. Gommer himself was said to have overcome one particularly severe March depression by seizing a tambourine and performing for his astounded community a peasant dance, half Morris, half Basque. No record was kept of where the tambourine came from or of the quality of Gommer's dancing; the story, like the Clang Bird story, was properly part of Thomasite oral tradition.

Though few were aware of it, however, the Clang Bird story existed in the written tradition as well. St. Gommer was an unwell man and had had occasion to make many dying remarks, the least fortunate of which concerned the Clang Bird.

He had been lying on his simple pallet of straw, coughing horribly. All at once he had stopped and, propping himself up on one bony elbow, he'd gazed above the heads of those around him and fixed his eyes upon some far-off moment in time. ". . . créature rare," he said, "l'Oiseau Clangale fait au vol des larges mouvements concentriques qui se rétrécissent de plus en plus et d'une rapidité si vertigineuse qu'il disparait clangalement, ô merveille terrestre, par le moyen de son cul. C'est seulement par la sainte volonté du bon Dieu que cet oiseau d'outre-mer existe toujours."*

His Brothers at the deathwatch were silent, uncertain what immediate application the remark might have, but dazzled by its possibilities. The secretary of the Order duly recorded the offending words and they were included finally in a manuscript volume, *Novissima Verba,* which St. Gommer's successor decreed as joined to the office of Superior General, much as the crown jewels were joined to the office of King. No future Superior General ever felt the urge to make the last words of St. Gommer commonly available. The book rested on a shelf in Rome, side by side with the condemned writings of Voltaire, Rousseau, and other heretics. Though it was rarely consulted, its spine was cracked and the book opened automatically to "créature rare, l'Oiseau Clangale. . . ." The passage was dated, not surprisingly, 1717, March.

Over the two-and-a-half centuries following St. Gom-

*The Clang Bird is a rare creature that flies in ever decreasing circles at ever increasing speeds until, with a terrible clang, it disappears up its own ass. It is only because of the will of God that the Clang Bird is not yet extinct.

dered. She was taken by the simple eloquence of Jesus, and was amused that far from practicing Catholic logic, He seemed to practice no logic at all, preferring, whenever He was questioned, to dodge the issue. Thus, confronted with pointed questions about the woman taken in adultery and about rendering taxes to Caesar, He ignored the questions and instead of answers offered irrelevant put-downs that made very different points of His own. It was clever and it was economical, but it was not logic, certainly not Catholic logic. She felt He was a man she would have liked.

Encouraged, she read St. Paul but disliked him at once, a hysteric, pushing people around in the name of Jesus. She suspected it was with Paul that the special pleading had begun.

She discussed her reading with Reginald and was surprised at his bland acceptance of the Gospels; he had never seen Jesus as a particularly original figure, he was merely the Son of God, the Messiah, the . . .

"*Merely* the Son of God," she said.

"Well, you know," he said.

Natalie gave up on St. Paul and went back to the Gospels. The thought struck her that nowhere in these four books was there a mention of philosophy, nowhere the grand abstractions that gave an illusion of substance to so many lectures she had sat through; Jesus would never have made it at the University. He was concrete, practical. If He was saying what she thought He was saying—you don't love the Father unless you show it by helping other people—then He was terribly radical as well.

She asked Reginald if this was, as a matter of fact, what Jesus was talking about. He gave her a long theological answer that came down to yes and no. But he also had begun to read the Gospels again.

Whatever Jesus was saying, she concluded, He was ruthless about it, uncompromising. And it didn't involve having packs of money, let alone the securities, the cars, the fur coats that Christians were so fond of. And what about the Thomasites, she thought, with their bottles of wine and their high living? Reginald shrugged and said she was right.

"But how can you say that and live the way you do?" she said.

"You've got to face the fact that you're human," he said, "and human life, of its nature, involves some compromise."

"Does it?"

"Yes, it does." But he knew there was a time when he had not thought so.

As March moved into April, Reginald took Natalie to dinner at Barney's. Doris was there with Barbie. When they were leaving the restaurant, Doris passed by quickly with a little hand wave and a "Hiya," but Barbie said "Well, hell-o" to Natalie in what seemed to be a pointed way. Natalie was upset afterward and, back at her apartment, Reginald held her in his arms to comfort her. Inevitably, they ended up going to bed. They made love tenderly but almost automatically and afterward lay there silent, staring at the ceiling.

"We shouldn't have done that."

"No, we shouldn't have."

Neither of them spoke for a few minutes.

"Are we still friends?" His voice was hesitant.

"It was only self-indulgence."

"Yes."

"I see what they mean by sin. It's not the sex part at all."

"But we can still be friends."

"I don't know," she said.

For the time being they remained friends, and the process set in motion was accelerated. Natalie began to study the Dutch Catechism and to browse through the Thomas More Book Shop where she bought books on Scripture and the sacraments and the meaning of the Eucharist. So much of it was fraudulent, she thought, so much of it riddled with Catholic logic.

Nevertheless, despite her reading and despite her aversion to almost every outward manifestation of the Church, her peculiar detached intelligence was leading her into Catholicism. She knew it, she had seen it coming. And she watched, understanding, unable to prevent what was happening to her.

As Natalie moved toward a religion for which she had little respect, Doris moved steadily away from it.

In the days following her night with Malfoof, Doris formulated a principle on sex. Going to bed with Malfoof was all right, but going to bed with anyone else was out, unless of course there were a pressing reason. Offhand, she could not think of what a pressing reason might be, but her new openmindedness insisted on providing for the possibility.

George, in any case, was not a pressing reason. He was insistent, following her about the campus and phoning at all hours of the night. He was almost charming in his frantic need for her attention and in his boyish jealousy of Malfoof, but clearly he was no exception to her principle. And besides, George was still a priest.

"Please let me come over," he would insist. "I only want to talk."

"You're a priest, George. You shouldn't be dirty."

"I'm going to leave," he would whisper in a frenzy, checking the phone booth door to make sure it was shut, "I'm going to leave very soon. Can I come over for just a few minutes?"

"Not now, George, Malfoof is here."

Malfoof was often there, lolling on the harem pillows now scattered about the living room or doing the Canadian Air Force Exercises together with Doris. Malfoof found them amusing and, more than that, a helpful preparation for an evening of delights. He had bought her an immense Persian carpet to replace the crimson shag rug which offended his Eastern taste and often they would spend the night in the living room, moving from the cushions to the carpet, stopping to nibble dates or figs, and then returning to the cushions.

"Ya elbi," he would whisper.

"Binky. Silly old Binky."

"My fertile bough."

"Oh!"

"My bowl of curd, my well of sweet waters."

"Oh, God!"

God was not often in Doris' thoughts at this time nor were her days as a Sister of Divine Prudence. Her ten years in religion seemed now to have happened in some previous incarnation, to some other person altogether. For Doris the passions of the flesh and the passions of mind and spirit had at last become one. And she owed it all to Malfoof.

As March moved into April, Malfoof left his solitary suite in the Men's Dormitory and moved into Doris' apartment.

"It's economical this way," she said, and with the thought of all the money they were saving, she replaced the Danish modern with Mediterranean furniture, massive chests and chairs of ebony that were as black and shining as Malfoof himself. Money was no problem to either of them, for besides Daddy there was the tribe of Mihshay who, it turned out, supplied the oil that daddy had grown rich by importing.

Doris took Barbie to dinner at Barney's to explain the new household arrangements.

"It's really fab," she said, "I mean, with Malfoof I have a real existential relationship. It's person to person."

"It must be nice," Barbie said.

"I don't bother with church any more. It isn't relevant."

"I know what you mean." Barbie warmed to a topic she could at last talk about. She had heard enough about ecstatic nights with Malfoof. "The Church," she said, "has never understood women. Look at Molly Bloom."

"And the Lollipops. Well, there just doesn't seem to be any need. I mean, it's almost over, the war."

"Men don't understand."

On the way out of the restaurant they saw Reginald and Natalie having dinner. Doris felt about Reginald the way she felt about the Church, he was irrelevant to her new existential relationship, and she passed by quickly with a little hand wave. Barbie, however, went straight to the table and said "Well, hell-o" to Natalie in what seemed to be a pointed way. Doris would have thought Barbie's action strange if she had thought about Barbie at all, but nobody ever thought about Barbie, Natalie alone excepted.

A week before she said "hell-o" at the restaurant, Barbie had once again succeeded in getting Natalie alone. She had seen the long black hair and the miniskirt disappearing into Lawman Cafeteria, and though half the girls at the University had long black hair and miniskirts, she recognized Natalie at once. She joined her at the table where she was having coffee.

"Reginald is a priest, you know, and priests have vows." Barbie was not going to waste time with indirections.

Natalie sipped her coffee.

"If he falls in love with you, you'll be responsible for destroying his whole life's work. He's a priest, you know. He belongs to the Church."

Natalie looked at her watch. She thought she might scream.

"Men don't understand women anyway. Priests don't. *We* would understand each other."

"What is it that lies at the center of your religion?" Natalie asked, her tone revealing nothing.

"Love," Barbie said, adding quickly, "and purity."

Natalie had good reason to think about Barbie and so, as it turned out, did George. It was Barbie who gave him the news about Malfoof's moving in with Doris, and she omitted none of the infuriating details—the harem pillows, the circles under Doris' eyes, the Mihshay tribe wallowing in oil money.

George was distraught.

"I can't go on," he said, "I've got to talk to someone."

"You can talk to me, George," Barbie said.

"I want to tell all."

"Tell me all, George."

George told her all, though in his version "all" came down to having once slept with a girl—"Doris," he admitted, and hung his head—and now he was obsessed by the thought of her. Barbie listened, nodding and clucking sympathetically; she knew how it was.

"I too have loved," she said.

George was shocked. He had never thought of Barbie going to bed with anyone; then again, he had never thought of Barbie at all.

"You?"

"It's true," she said.

George waited what he considered a discreet amount of time and then his curiosity got the better of him.

"Who with?"

"It's embarrassing."

"You can tell me."

"I'm not sure, George."

"Come on," he said. "I told you."

"Well, all right. But I don't know what you'll think of me. With Malfoof and Natalie."

Malfoof and Natalie. George could not absorb the information. Malfoof and Natalie, he said to himself over and over, Malfoof and Natalie. He still could not absorb it.

"You mean Malfoof and Reginald," he said.

"No, I mean Natalie. They look alike, Natalie and Reginald, have you ever noticed that? But I mean Natalie."

"And you've gone to bed with *both* of them?"

It was Barbie's turn to be shocked.

"Sins of thought, George, sins of desire."

Malfoof and Natalie. George began to give Barbie a great deal of thought. She really was, he reflected, a most unusual girl.

Reginald, more than any of the others, found March a difficult month.

Reginald's intelligence was of a peculiar controlling sort that enabled him not only to understand what was happening to him but also, much more than in most men, to make it happen or not happen, as seemed best. Thus he had chosen the priestly vocation from purely intellectual considerations and afterward, for almost fourteen years, his will had gone along with that decision. Thus also he had known he might well fall in love with Natalie and, by refusing to focus his intelligence on the consequences of falling in love, he had gone ahead and done it. And so, waking that first morning with Natalie, he saw plainly to what he had come; several days passed before he saw where he might go.

In the meanwhile, he went back to the house on Oak Road and thought. Sex had never been a problem to him and hence he had never particularly desired it or missed it, but now that he had actually slept with Natalie he marveled that he had lived so long as a celibate. He was happy with what he had done. Off and on throughout the day he wanted to go to her apartment and begin all over again. He did not.

When a few days had passed, confession became a problem. Should he confess. And what should he say? What had happened between Natalie and himself was good and natural and in no way selfish; how could he then consider it a sin? And how could he confess if he did not think it was a sin? He decided to talk it over with Sean.

Sean's reaction was what Reginald had expected. He sat there nodding, as if Reginald had just told him that Skakespeare was a great playwright or that the University was a bore.

"Yeah," Sean said. "I see your problem. Look, why don't you do this–go to some confessor, anyone but Hitler, and tell him what you've done and that you don't consider it a sin but you know the Church does, and so you want to confess it as whatever it is in the eyes of God. That puts all the worry on God."

"I thought of that, Sean, but the trouble is that that doesn't resolve it for *me*. That's a compromise."

"You're human, Reg, even you, and humanity means—like it or not—a certain amount of compromise."

"Sounds shitty."

"It is shitty. As we walk down the bridle path of life, dear Father, God sees to it that all of us step in a little horseshit."

In the end, Reginald followed his advice.

Almost a week passed before he saw Natalie again and by that time she had decided to let him take the lead. She was not certain that she loved him—her discerning intelligence seemed always to collapse in the face of love—and so, for the moment, she left the disposal of their lives to him.

"We ought to wait," he said, "until I decide whether or not to leave the priesthood."

"That's good," she said, "that pleases me," though in fact it did not. She said so only to please Reginald.

Later she asked him what it was that lay at the heart of the Christian religion. When he had thought for a while he said, "Jesus Christ, I suppose, but it's all one. Yes, Jesus Christ." He had never really given the matter much reflection before, but that Sunday he preached about Christ as the balance point of the Christian religion. He had begun taking parish calls, hearing confessions on Saturday and preaching on Sunday. He had also begun to read the Gospels once again.

He perceived where Natalie's inquiries were leading her, but did nothing to encourage them. Faith was too heavy a burden to shift on to anyone else's back, he told himself, wondering if he were a heretic. He felt almost consoled by her obvious irritation in the presence of all things Catholic. And yet she pursued it, something, whatever it was she was after. Watching her, Reginald thought, it's as if she had to invent the language all over again. He began to see her less often, busy as he was with work in St. Mark's parish; he had joined the Big Brother program for a black boy from Roxbury and he was teaching French in the Cambridge Free School.

The less he saw Natalie, the more he realized he was genuinely in love with her. He had a constant ache beneath his ribcage and some nights in bed he would roll from side to side, his knees clasped to his chest, consumed with desire for her. Yet when he was with her, they were like old friends who shared common intellectual interests. There was affection between them, emotion even, but no romance. The relationship appeared on the surface to be as placid as it was rich.

Relationships within the community on Oak Road, however, were not placid and not rich. Sean and Hans were continually arguing, Hans invariably getting the worst of it, hampered as he was by his plodding mind and slow wit. Billy's confusion about life and all its varieties had become an annoyance to everyone. Jim was rarely home and, when he was, his professional competence and his personal imperturbability bothered the others almost as much as Hans' bungling and Billy's asking why.

But it was Reginald who became somehow the focus of

28

"I worry about her sometimes," Bob Moran said. He was referring to Doris who had just sailed by them with an airy wave.

"I used to. I don't any more," Barbie said. "Doris knows what she's doing."

"Does she?" It was not a challenge. He was merely surprised. "Maybe she does. Maybe I'm the one More and more I feel like I'm living on the periphery of things. Do you ever feel like that?"

She spotted George moping across the Yard. "I used to," she said, "I don't any more." He was going toward the library.

"Oh? How come?"

"I have to go now, Bob. I have to pick up some books." Barbie walked away from him, quickly, so that by the time she reached the library door she had caught up to George.

"Well, if it isn't himself," she said, and raised her eyebrows as if they shared some secret, or should.

the community's discontent. He was snappish, they said,
rude. "He's becoming the kind of priest," Sean said, "
everybody outside thinks is terrific and everybody who l
with him thinks is a son of a bitch." It was true that his l
silences had disappeared and in their place was an offh
unconcern, marked by shoulder shrugs and flippant
marks. When he was studying now, he did not want t
interrupted. Nor did he clean the house. "You crapped
you clean it," he once said to Jim, and nobody spoke
way to Jim. He had taken to telling people exactly wh
felt about what they said and did. Reg, good old Reg
ceased to be charming and there was considerable do
to whether he really was deep.

As for Reginald himself, he felt he had been summ
back to life and his only concern was to spend it lavish
would have been surprised to learn that the communi
begun to feel about him the way he had long felt abou

For a month and a half, then, Natalie groped to
Catholicism she did not want and Reginald toward a
hood he thought he had abandoned. March mov
April and they slept together for the second and la
and, after that, they chose their separate ways.

After much looking, Natalie found a priest she co
to, Father Claude, a Paulist in downtown Boston, a
him she began the hated instructions in the
faith. Reginald, loving her even more, chose the pr
for a second time, conscious that this choice, too,
the wrong one. He shrugged and read the Scriptu
more.

29

Sean shifted from foot to foot. He was uncomfortable with his message and Reginald was no help, sitting there with his book still open in front of him, his finger keeping his place on the page.

"I'm checking," Sean said. Reginald looked at him blankly. "I just thought I'd mention it to you."

"Checking?"

"Out. Of the Thomasites. And for that matter, out of the University as well."

Despite the almost universal belief that Sean would not last till ordination, Reginald was surprised. He closed his book and thought for a moment. Then suddenly he felt pleased at the rightness of Sean's decision; some men should get out before the damage is done. He could visualize Sean at sixty, a cantankerous drunk, the terror of the recreation room, raging about what he could have been if only Superiors had given him a chance. He could hear the bitterness in his voice, see the scotch lines carved in his face. Looking up, he was surprised to see Sean, twenty-five, skinny and healthy and expectant, waiting for his response.

"Great!" Reginald said. "Congratulations."

Sean grinned. "Real broken up, I see."

Later that afternoon, for no reason he could think of—except that they were friends, sort of, they had shared a hundred cups of coffee, she would want to know—he went to Natalie's apartment.

"Sean! What a nice surprise. And you've had your hair cut."

"I'm leaving," he said.

"No, come in. I'll make some coffee."

"Leaving the Thomasites."

"And well done, too. Come in and tell me all about it."

They talked for the remainder of the afternoon—God, women were wonderful, Sean kept thinking—and he left only because it was well past dinner time. Only much later did it occur to him that, of course, he should have asked her to have dinner with him. By then, a month had passed and he was living in Boston, working for WHDH-TV. She would probably think he was boring, think he was dull, think he was foolish if he were to call her now. Natalie Meyer Kelly flashed through his mind. God, he *was* foolish.

Leaving her apartment, he shook her hand.

"Maybe we'll run into one another again sometime," he said.

"I'd like that," Natalie said. "I hope we do."

"Ayni," he said, kissing her eyes. "Ya elbi."

"Mahboub."

"My fountain of delights."

"Ya habibi." Doris had memorized certain Arabic endearments which Malfoof was able to translate from her Greenwhich version back into acceptable Arabic.

He made gnawing noises now as he bit her softly on the breasts and buttocks, the ribcage and the stomach. She was rubbery, no question, but to Malfoof she was a Turkish delight and he was insatiable.

"What am I called?"

"Mahboub."

"No, what am I called?"

"Binky. My silly old Binky."

Malfoof went quite out of his head. And then, as always, she tumbled down some emotional cliff. It was happening again, she thought, Kate Millett notwithstanding, and her head snapped back, spun away from her, and only their joined bodies remained.

She let out a slow, high, piercing wail, as she imagined Lebanese women did at such moments.

"It is highly sufficient," Malfoof said a long time later.

March had been a poor month for the production of molotov cocktails, but with spring the McReedys were back at work again. They had a new incentive. Reginald had brought his Little Brother, a black from Roxbury, to visit the house on Oak Road. A nigger in their own house! Francis bought a second can of gasoline that afternoon.

Michael was bored. He was never allowed to do any of the exciting things. Lately, Francis wouldn't even let him smoke in the cellar.

"How come I don't ever get to try out one? How come you're always the one who gets to trash the handball courts."

"Because you're a little shit, that's how come. And don't smoke down here, I told you."

"I'll smoke if I want."

"I'll break your ass."

He put out the cigarette.

They had actually had a small fire once when Michael flicked his cigarette ash into a soup dish that contained some lighter fluid. Francis smothered it easily with an old bathmat he kept for Judy Malocha but afterwards he refused to let Michael smoke in the cellar.

Nonetheless Michael still lit up, just to infuriate his brother, and twice he had pretended to throw his cigarette into the can of gasoline. It was a way of making time pass.

"He has a sense of humor, you know. God does."

Turning that proposition over in her mind, Natalie found it was one of the few to which she could give unconditioned assent.

"I still don't like it," she said. "Not the structure, not the Pope, and certainly not nuns."

"No one likes nuns," Father Claude said. "You don't have to like any of it; I don't much like it myself. But you have to be easy with it, let God get at you in his own way. That may mean, for you, not entering the Church at all."

"I'm entering," Natalie said, "but I don't like it."

"One has to study the old to understand the new," Hans said aloud and repeated it twice more. He had turned in desperation to his memory book.

Winter had been filled with a new anxiety for Hans. His monthly sting of the flesh had attacked him with a casual arbitrariness he could not account for. When he least expected it, sometimes only a week after the last damning act, he would find his hands creeping down there with that filthy life of their own, eager to fumble and push, to do their worst.

"One has to study the old to understand the new," he said again, and stumbled off to an icy shower, where up until the last moment he prayed to God for deliverance.

"Come on to bed," he said.

"No, George, it wouldn't be right."

He nuzzled her.

"Sex is never right except in marriage." One way or another, Barbie always managed to raise the question of marriage.

"You're still a nun," he said. "You can't get married."

"You're still a priest," she said.

George thought of Doris, probably cradled in the arms of that black heathen.

"Come on to bed," he said.

"And lose the pearl of great price?" she said.

Barbie had her own thoughts and desires.

". . . not only divine, but human as well. Not God dressed up in flesh for a thirty-three-year charade, but a real man.

He had sore feet and calloused hands; He wept real tears over Lazarus, His friend; and He loved Mary Magdalen, even in her sin."

The congregation stared. It was a nice change for a Sunday to hear a sermon by a handsome young man, with a golden beard yet. They all nudged one another when Reginald began to speak; he had that educated way about him, a Thomasite no doubt.

"Furthermore He encouraged her to love Him, even though the neighbors must have been horrified and even though He must have sensed the risk He took of breaking her heart." Reginald paused. "And we, what do we risk?"

Reginald had prepared his sermon carefully, writing and rewriting it, memorizing it, pacing up and down his room until he had it word for word. But always his mind would go blank after "what do we risk?" He tossed all night, and when he rose in the morning, he wrote on a filing card, "I risk never becoming a whole man. Celibacy asks of me that I surrender to Christ all hope of ever possessing or being possessed in love. My love must be scattered around for anyone who wants it. I can never expect a return of love except from God, and He loves in mysterious ways. I risk being deformed by loneliness. It's a risk I'll take, not tomorrow and forever, but today and today and one day at a time." When he had written this, he tore the card into small pieces and, for once, went smiling to breakfast.

Preaching now, he said, "And we, what do we risk?" and found his mind shifting to the torn filing card and then back to his prepared text. He wound through seven minutes to his conclusion. "The raising of Jairus' daughter from the dead demonstrates the power of love and forewarns scoffers that at the Last Judgment we shall be asked, each one of us, Whom have you raised from the dead? Whom have you loved back to life?" He was sweating profusely. He paused for almost a minute to let his audience grow uncomfortable with the question, and then he made the sign of the Cross.

Afterward in the sacristy he was folding the vestments and saying to himself, I can do it today, today I'm able, but I can promise nothing for tomorrow, when one of the altar boys told him there was a woman to see him. He closed his eyes; he knew the kind of woman who haunted sacristies.

"My land," she said, "I just had to tell you I could listen to you all day." Reginald smiled, kindly. "You've got the nicest voice. Just like my nephew, the Jesuit." And she went on and on about the Jesuits and her nephew and how she had risked all for her Church.

30

For Reginald, that spring was badly out of focus. The turmoil in his private life seemed to be reflected in the cataclysmic things happening around him. Peace parades turned into trashing expeditions. Home-made bombs exploded in closets of public buildings. Agnew was spouting alliterative denunciations and there were riots on campuses everywhere and then suddenly, terribly, there was the invasion of Cambodia. That was on the last day of April.

Reginald saw the headlines as he cut through the Square. "Cambodia Invaded"; this was somehow the worst betrayal. The war was winding down at last, troops were being withdrawn, further protests seemed mere self-indulgence. And now here was a whole new war beginning. It was insane. It was wanton. Reginald sank deep into one of his silences.

He had been silent for over twenty-four hours when the phone rang. It was Doris asking him to come over and talk with some friends about the Cambodian invasion. Reginald said he didn't know if he could make it.

"Everyone's coming," Doris said. "Natalie is. Why don't you pick her up and come together?"

"Why not," he said.

A few minutes later, Doris was on the phone to Natalie.

"Everyone's coming," she said. "Reg thought he'd pick you up and you can come over together."

Natalie clenched her teeth and frowned. She said she would be there.

Reginald and Natalie were the last to arrive. In the gloom they could pick out Barbie enthroned in a high-backed velvet chair and George, looking anxious, in its companion. Malfoof beamed at them from an enormous sofa. The floor seemed littered with bodies which turned out to be Bob Moran and several Christian Brothers reclining on cushions.

Reginald and Natalie stood at the door, squinting into the shadowy room.

"It's hard to see at first," Doris said.

"Well, it's certainly Eastern," Reginald said, blinking.

"Mmmm, yes," Natalie said.

Candles burned on the long wooden table and on the massive chests which concealed the stereo speakers. An iron brazier flickered against the far wall. The television glowed, soundless. There was no other illumination.

"Down to business," Doris said, suddenly efficient. "You know everybody, I think. Malfoof, George and Gunnie—Barbie, I mean—and Bob Moran. And you know the Christian Brothers." No one was sure of their names and they seemed not to mind their anonymity, so there was no point in trying to sort them out. "Well," she said brightly, "here we are."

Natalie and Reginald sat on the sofa next to Malfoof. Natalie wished she had not come. Reginald began to feel the first stirrings of anger.

"Cambodia is what we've got to talk about," Doris began, "and all the lying and hypocrisy of a government that's committed to total dominance of the Far East. Nixon has pretended he's winding down the war when actually he's waging new ones." Here she settled herself on a cushion at Malfoof's feet, her purple gown spreading in thick folds on the carpet. "So who wants to begin?"

"What we're going to *do* about it is the big thing," Bob Moran said.

"Right," Doris said.

"Right," all the Christian Brothers said together.

"We've got to take action," Doris said. "The Koran tells us, 'God would not prevent you from doing battle with those who have chased you from your homes.' "

Malfoof beamed and tickled her ear.

"But we haven't been driven from our homes," Barbie said.

"The point is clear just the same. The South Vietnamese have and it's our job to put them back."

"But isn't that intervention too, just like the war?" The Christian Brother who asked the question was genuinely puzzled. The others glared at him.

Reginald and Natalie shifted uneasily on the sofa.

George looked from Natalie to Doris and then to Barbie. And then back to Doris. She was so sexy and so rich.

"We're all agreed about how wrong the war is. And we're agreed that the Cambodian invasion is an outrage." Bob's cheek began to twitch as he cleared away the others' foggy thinking. "What we've got to decide is how we can most dramatically and publicly register our protest. Letters to our Congressmen have failed. Peace marches have failed. It's time now to take action and the only question is what action we ought to take. And then we've got to take it."

Everyone was silent. Everyone was impressed.

Bob looked to Reginald for approval and slowly everyone else did the same.

But to Reginald, it was all preposterous: the room, the people, the talk. He could not get rid of the idea that they were playing roles in a film. This lavish ridiculous room was a movie set, Doris was an Arabian actress from Greenwich, Connecticut. Before they could say one honest word, a director would have to shout "cut and print"; only then could they return to the business of being themselves.

He was angry and now he began to feel guilty about being angry. And yet, he thought, the childishness of this playing at revolution! None of them were revolutionaries; they were only bored and lazy. And Doris the worst of all. Rich and spoiled and talking about exploiting the Far East. If she wanted to see capitalistic exploitation at its most dramatic, she had only to look to Daddy. His anger fixed on her. She ought to be told. She ought to face herself as the ridiculous figure she was. He lowered his head until he could get control of his feelings.

Everyone waited. Reg was going to come up with one of his profound insights.

"What do you think, Reg?"

"I think you ought to decide whether you want to play harem or revolution, and then get on with it."

He stood for a moment facing Doris, his mouth working, his hands clenched. And then, unable or unwilling to say what he was thinking, he slammed out of the room. Through the door they heard him say, "Jesus Christ," and then he was gone.

They were dumbfounded. Charming Reg. Wonderful Reg. Storming out of the meeting just when they were getting somewhere. It didn't make sense.

". . . and naturally, I'll keep this confidential," Natalie was saying as she moved toward the door. "I'm afraid I'm not very revolutionary."

Doris had risen from the cushions and was seeing Natalie out when all at once Natalie placed her palm against Doris' cheek and looked into her eyes, saying, "I'm sorry. I am." Doris was stunned; it was as if Natalie knew something she herself did not. She stood at the door and watched Natalie down the stairs.

The only sound in the room was the sputter of the brazier in the corner. No one wanted to be first to break the silence.

"Gosh," Bob said finally. "I seem to have broken up the party."

"No. No, not at all," Doris responded automatically, her mind still on Natalie. "What you said was very nice. It was very true."

The room went silent once more.

"Well, maybe it's time to be going. It's getting late anyhow." Bob stood up and began to rub his knees. "Getting old," he said.

"I've got it!" George, staring at Doris, had been seized by inspiration. "Let's do it now. Let's go straight to a draft board and trash it now. Right away."

They all looked at one another in alarm. Raiding a draft board office had been proposed and discussed so often during the past months that it had taken on an air of unreality. Something you might read about in the newspapers. Certainly not something you actually went out and did.

Doris began to smile.

"What do you say?" George pressed his advantage. He could feel himself swelling under her approving eyes. "Let's do it right now."

"You're marvelous!" she said, and threw her arms around him. "Absolutely fab!"

"You are, George. Just fab!" Barbie took him by the arm, gently easing Doris out of range.

George glowed with the feeling of responsibility. He shot his arms into the air and made V signs in imitation of President Nixon. "Take me to your leader," he said. "Come on, gang," and, hearts high, he led them off into the night to commit their first federal crime.

But out on the street they began to argue about whose car they should use.

"Doris'," Bob said. "I've only signed mine out until midnight."

Doris did not agree. "I think it should be Bob's," she said. "I think you should force the Jesuits to be involved, to commit themselves on the war."

"They are involved," Bob said. "Look at the Catonsville Nine. Look at the Chicago Eight. The Jesuits have more men in jail than any other religious order."

The Christian Brothers nodded. Sadly, what Bob said was true.

George, unimpressed by the number of imprisoned Jesuits and anxious not to lose his sudden leadership, told them he'd decided they would take both cars. Period. "Besides," he said, "we're attracting attention here." A man walking his dog turned to glance at Doris in her purple velvet gown. "See?" George said.

The two cars roared away.

Shortly after, they rendezvoused at MacDonald's. It seemed none of them knew just where the local draft board office was located.

"We could ask someone," Doris suggested, "we could ask a cop."

"A cop! Are you crazy!"

"Oh, gosh, that's right. I'm so dumb sometimes."

Malfoof, beside her, stroked her knee. "Ayni," he said, "my butterfly."

One of the Christian Brothers said he knew where there was a draft board, but it was up near Beverly. No one liked the idea of trashing an office that wasn't in Boston proper, but George insisted that any office was better than no office at all. And so they tore off in their cars once more, munching the Big Macs Doris had bought for everyone.

The drive to the draft board office was interminable. It was up a side street, the Christian Brother insisted, a converted grocery store that was now divided into a real estate office on one side and the draft board office on the other. Or at least that is where it had been five years earlier when he had gone to be reclassified.

"It's right down this street," he said. "Turn left. Turn *left.*"

Bob swung the car abruptly to the left, Doris careening along behind him, and the two cars drove the length of the tree-lined street. There was no sign of a converted grocery store.

"It's after midnight," Bob said. "I'm supposed to have the car back by now."

"It's down *this* street. I remember now. Take the next right."

There was no sign of a converted grocery store there either.

Behind them Doris honked three times, the signal for a conference.

"Pull in the first place you can," she said. "We must be lost."

On the next corner there was a graveled parking place in front of a converted grocery store. Bob pulled in and Doris parked beside him. By accident they had found the draft board office.

And now, after all this, they discovered they had nothing with them with which to force the damned door.

George threw himself against it and hurt his shoulder. The door did not budge.

"God," he said. "In the movies they always fly open."

"A crowbar," Doris suggested. "The thing you change a tire with that picks off the hubcaps. You could pry it open."

George inserted the metal bar and, gingerly, began to pull on it. There was a cracking sound as the wood splintered. He stopped.

"What's the matter?"

"The wood's breaking."

"My God, it is."

They all crowded around to get a better look at the splintered door frame.

On his knees, staring at the raw slivers of wood, George suddenly realized what he was doing. This is a crime, he thought, people go to jail for this. Sweat began to come out on his forehead. He stood up.

"This is crazy," he said, but stopped when he saw them all looking at him. Was he a coward? Did he merely talk a good game? He looked at Doris. "It's crazy trying to get the door open with this thing. What we need is something thin and slippery like a credit card or those Do Not Disturb signs they always rob hotels with. What we need is. . . ." He went on talking compulsively; anything to get his mind off the consequences of what they were doing.

"I've got it," Bob said, "this is so cool." He sprinted to the Jesuit car and returned in a moment waving a thin strip of white plastic. "Look. An inch and a half wide, a foot long, it's perfect." With a little bow he presented it to George.

"A Roman collar! Bob, you're a genius." Doris squeezed his arm and giggled.

Despairing, George sank to his knees and began to work the collar between the door and the frame.

"Have you got it?"

"Does it fit?"

"I'm trying. Goddamn it, I'm trying."

His hands were trembling so much he could not control them. He pushed at the collar and twisted it back and forth, trying to force it into the narrow crack.

"How's it coming?"

"Push it easier, George. Sort of slide it."

The collar twisted suddenly and fell from his shaking hands.

"Look!" he said, furious. "Everybody get back in the damned cars and just wait till I've got this done. I can't work with all of you breathing down my neck." Chastened, they began moving to the cars. "Except Doris. You stay here to, uh, hand me tools."

He tried again. The collar buckled and snapped free.

"It's because your hands are shaking," Doris said.

"They're not shaking."

"Sure they are. Just look."

"I'm doing this for you," he said, accusingly.

"Me?"

"I don't give a damn about draft boards. It's for you."

"Try the collar again, George."

"Well, don't you have anything to say? About what I just said?"

"Here, let me try it."

She took the collar from him and with ease inserted it between the door and the frame. George tried to snatch the collar back from her but she pushed him away. He tried again and this time in their struggle the collar tripped the lock and, to their surprise, the door swung open.

"You *did* it," she said, hoping to mend his feelings. "Oh,

George, that's marv."

"For you," he said, but it was too late to pursue the topic because the others had come running from the cars.

They entered the office on tiptoe.

"It's pitch black," Doris said in a whisper.

"Dusky," Malfoof said, picking up her whisper. "Black is for Panthers."

Bob lit a match. It flared up for a second, startling everyone, and then burned just long enough for them to have a quick look around. No question; the draft board office was a distinct disappointment. Two desks, a wall of filing cases, a door to a back room.

"There's a light switch right next to you, Barbie."

"But we can't have light. They'll see us."

"No. No lights."

They stood silent in the darkness.

"Why are we whispering?"

They laughed, self-conscious.

"Maybe if I leave the door open we can see by the light outside," George said. As he opened the door, a wedge of light spread across a corner of the room. "That should be enough, don't you think?" He looked outside; it was too late to run.

"That's perfect."

Again they stood silent. Nobody knew just how to begin.

"Well, let's start," Doris said. "Everybody take a file drawer and go to it."

They waited, watching her.

"This looks like what we want," she said.

She lifted the long thin drawer completely out of the filing case and placed it on one of the desks.

"There's not much on here," she said, reading quickly through the three-by-five card. She read another and then a third. "I guess this is what we're after, though."

She took a handful of cards and tried to tear them.

"Too many. I'll try it with just three."

She squared off the three cards and, with a quick strong motion, tore them in half. The sound was electric. She looked from the torn cards to the faces around her. Even in the dark room she could tell they were all staring at her. She looked back at the torn cards and then at her hands. Never in her life had she deliberately destroyed anything.

"It's got to be done," she said. "Each of these represents an innocent life being fed to the wolves of imperialism."

She tore the cards into quarters.

"It's got to be done."

"Right," Bob said. He joined her at the desk and tore a card in half. "Every card torn is a life saved."

In a moment everyone was tearing cards except George and Malfoof. George was exploring the back room. Malfoof was standing by the door, wringing his hands.

"Come on, Malfoof," Bob said, "join the crowd."

"I am here for my ayni. I cannot tear some cards."

"Here. You pile them in threes and I'll tear them," Barbie said. "We'll be a team."

"I will pile, but I will not tear."

"You've got beautiful hands," Barbie said, her mind

wandering for a moment from the tearing of draft cards.

The Christian Brothers were attacking the larger files where the piling and tearing required more strenuous effort. Everyone worked in silence and, given the blacked-out condition of the room, with a remarkable degree of efficiency. There was the general feeling that they were at last accomplishing something.

George returned to the group.

"There's a cabinet in the back room," he said to Doris. "Come and take a look at it."

She went with him.

"It's pitch black in here, George," she said. And then in a whisper, "What are you doing? For heaven's sake, George, stop that."

He had pinned her against the filing cabinet and was caressing her plump left buttock, his pelvis thrust hard against hers.

"Let me," he whispered, and moved his hand up to her breast.

"Stop it," she said, and when he did not, "I'll have Malfoof break your arm."

George continued to clutch at her.

"Or cut off your little thing," she said, momentarily inspired.

George winced and pulled away as if he had been stabbed.

Next door there was a loud retching sound and then a scramble in the dark. Doris threw off the deflated George and rushed into the other room where Bob was bent over a wastebasket. Everyone was gathered around him.

"He's throwing up," Barbie said.

"What's the matter?" Doris said. "Are you all right?"

"Yes, of course," Bob said, and threw up again.

He had been stacking and tearing happily, thinking of how his fellow Jesuits would now refer to him as one of the Beverly Eight, the newspaper articles that would appear, the actual court case in which they could finally argue the legality of the war. He had been happy. Then all at once it came to him that this was his ordination year. Superiors would never allow him to be ordained if they heard about his tearing up draft cards. His ordination would be postponed. His family would be disgraced. At this point he had looked into the wastebasket to assess the damage done.

"Oh God," he said, and threw up.

"You need air. Come on outside."

Leaning against the door, his face twitching, he said, "The dinner must have gotten to me. We had mystery meat for dinner."

"We should go," George said. "Poor Bob is sick."

"But there's still all those files. We can't leave the place like this. We've hardly done anything."

"I don't know, I think we've done quite a lot. More than most people ever do."

"Yes, but you can't live relatively. 'Being neither hot nor cold, I shall vomit you out of my mouth.' Apocalypse."

Bob went white once again.

"We should have poured blood on the files."

"Blood?"

"Chicken blood or some kind of blood. It's the symbolic part that matters."

"Ink. We could use ink."

"What's symbolic about ink?"

"Nothing, but at least it will muck up the files. We simply can't leave them this way."

Everyone searched for a bottle of ink. There wasn't any. They found typewriter cleaner and a small bottle of glue but these didn't go very far.

"Let's just tip all the files on to the floor."

"Good thinking."

They worked feverishly, tipping file drawers, scattering papers, kicking file cards about the room. Within ten minutes, they had accomplished their mission. The little office was a shambles.

George, crestfallen, was the first to leave, saying he would drive poor Bob home in the Jesuit car. Barbie and the Christian Brothers went with him. Malfoof and Doris, left behind, stood at the door gazing into the room.

There were papers everywhere. Empty filing drawers stood on end all over the room. The desks were heaped with torn cards. One wastebasket lay on its side, stained with Bob's vomit.

"It had to be done," Doris said and closed the door neatly behind her. The lock clicked back into place.

"It had to be done," she said again, and throwing her arms around Malfoof, she began to cry quietly against his chest.

Malfoof held her, his nursing dove, his sparrow, who felt obliged to do such hard things. It was highly sufficient.

31

Afterward, when they thought back to the spring of 1970, what always came to mind first was the evening they spent at Reginald's house. Their raid on the draft board became only one of several indelible memories provided by the first two weeks of May—memories of a marriage, a death, a federal crime—and later all of them agreed that what most marked the spring was the evening of the fifth of May.

On the first of May, Doris had summoned the Lollipops to her apartment.

In the earliest hours of the second of May they had raided the draft board office.

For the next day or two they did not see one another. They were embarrassed. Perhaps the raid had been a foolish mistake.

On the fourth of May, the killings at Kent State convinced them they had done well to destroy the draft files. They met at Doris' once again and agreed to turn themselves in to the FBI at the rally in Washington and thus bring national attention both to the rationality of their behavior and the irrationality of the war.

On the fifth of May, they all met at Reginald's house.

On the eighth of May, despite everything that had happened on the fifth, Doris and Malfoof, George and Barbie flew to Washington to protest the war and to turn themselves in to the FBI. Bob Moran could not accompany them; he had been resting in a retreat house in Lenox for the past three days. It was on the flight to Washington that Doris told George and Barbie of her plans to marry Malfoof at the end of the semester—providing they were not all in jail, of course.

On the ninth of May, George and Barbie were married by a dissident Washington priest. They stood within earshot of President Nixon as he made midnight chat with a group of sulky young people gathered at the Lincoln Memorial. George and Barbie were without benefit of blood tests or license, but the priest was standing there and it seemed a good idea at the time and so they married. It was a beautiful way of protesting the Nixon hypocrisy, everyone felt. After the wedding they tried to turn themselves in to the police but, even though police were everywhere, they could find none willing to arrest them.

On the twelfth of May, Reginald was arrested and charged with conspiracy, the possession of weapons of war, and a long list of other crimes which, if he were found guilty, would have caused him to spend the larger part of his life in jail. Hans Berger, to everyone's surprise, was named his fellow-conspirator.

They might have recalled any of these things, and certain of them—George, for instance—had reason to, for his marriage obliged him to all the hardships he had never been able to bear as a Thomasite. Yet, afterward, despite the many disasters both political and personal, what all of them recalled first about the spring of 1970 was that evening of the fifth of May when they gathered—for the last time, so it turned out—at Reginald's house, in the protest community on Oak Road.

32

On that evening of the fifth of May, Reginald was at his desk thinking about all that had happened during the previous five days. His phone rang. He was tired and he let it ring for a full minute.

He was embarrassed. Perhaps he should not have stalked out of Doris' apartment with quite so much flourish. And yet he hadn't been able to help it. There she was spouting her revolutionary clichés, while she sprawled on cushions in a place that must have cost Daddy, and his employees, a Greenwich mean income. It was absurd, the whole Lollipop thing was absurd. Nevertheless, he reflected, it had not been necessary to tell her she should decide whether she wanted to play harem or revolution and then get on with it.

He had felt a little embarrassed, even at the time. The next day, luckily, was Saturday and he had been able to salve his conscience by telling each of his penitents to say three Our Fathers for the innocent people of Cambodia, a penance received for the most part in shocked silence. The FBI agent assigned to Reginald returned to the confessional three times, scandalized that a priest should use the sacrament for political purposes. He was scandalized even further the next morning—he was a conventional devout Catholic—when Reginald preached on war crimes and the innocent bystanders who sacrifice their innocence by merely standing by. Reginald himself was pleased with the sermon, particularly so the next day, when the killings at Kent State seemed to him to confirm his judgment that a right-wing hysteria was taking over the country.

On the evening of the fifth of May he was at his desk, thinking about these things, when the phone rang. He let it go on ringing for a full minute and then, fearing it would be one of the Lollipop crowd, he picked up the receiver.

"We're at Doris' place," Bob Moran said. "We've been talking about certain things, you know, and there are certain things we'd like to tell you about." His voice was heavy with innuendo; you could never tell what wires were being tapped.

"I can't get away tonight, Bob. I've got a call coming,

long distance, and I have to stick around till it comes."

There was a whispered conference at the other end of the line while Reginald prayed over and over, please God, don't let them think of coming over here.

"Perfect, Reg, we'll come over there. See you in a few minutes."

"Right."

As had happened more than once lately, Reginald found himself annoyed with God.

"But I can't stand those people," Natalie said, "they're just this side of being lunatics."

There was a strange clicking sound on the phone.

"Well, I'm not all that wild about them either, but they're coming over and I'm stuck with them."

"You shouldn't let them come over. Why did you say they could come over? You should have said no."

"Well, to tell the truth, I felt embarrassed about what I said to Doris and I thought I'd make peace."

"Yes, you did go a bit far."

"Come over." There was only silence on the phone. "Please."

Natalie ground her teeth, a peculiar and not unattractive habit she had picked up during instructions from Father Claude. It was a physical gesture that invariably preceded the submission of her will.

"Oh God," she said, "all right."

"Hold on." A siren shrieked outside his window and, for

an insane moment, Reginald thought of police and wire-tapping and all the paranoid persecutions that were the Lollipops' daily bread. But the siren belonged to an ambulance sent to pick up Grandma Shea. "It was just an ambulance," he said. "Come as soon as you can."

Natalie hung up and Reginald was about to when, once again, he heard the strange clicking on the line. I'm getting just like them, he thought, and to fight against the creeping paranoia he said into the receiver, "I hereby confess a conspiracy to overthrow the United States government and Herbert Hoover, in that order. Hans Berger is my accomplice. Ta-raaaa!" And he hung up then, satisfied.

Grandma Shea had been complaining about headaches ever since New Year's day. It was the Christmas tree, she said, with all those blinking lights that hurt her eyes. Too much television, the McReedys said. Then it was pains in her chest. Gas, they said. When finally she vomited blood and collapsed on the bathroom floor, they had no explanation. Cerebral hemorrhage, the doctor said, and summoned an ambulance.

As the orderlies carried her mother down the front stairs, Mrs. McReedy cried quietly into her handkerchief. It was always up to her, everything was. Fran was on duty, she was alone with the children, and now mother. . . . She blew her nose and stared at the white face on the stretcher. She couldn't bear the disgrace of having her mother in a rest home, but she couldn't bear taking care of an invalid either. Maybe mother would die, God rest her soul, she thought. Shaking her head sadly, she got into the ambulance. Everything was always up to her.

The ambulance had not yet pulled away from the curb when Francis was on the phone to Judy Malocha.

Everyone arrived at the same time.

Natalie had just turned into Oak Road, her back stiff, her teeth grinding, when a new Buick rocketed by her with Malfoof at the wheel. As she watched in disbelief, the car screeched to a halt, leaving rubber tracks on the blacktop, and at once, thrown into reverse, it roared back a few yards, scattering gravel and emitting clouds of exhaust, and then forward again. Priests and nuns, she thought, they're mad, they're dangerous.

The doors opened and Malfoof leaped out, grinning, "I am driving," he shouted to Natalie, "it is me." He helped Doris out of the car while George, not grinning at all, let Barbie shift for herself.

Malfoof was the only one visibly in high spirits. Doris looked festive in a harem dress of silver lamé by Pucci, but she felt it was wrong to actually feel festive and so she kept her desire for celebration decently concealed, though in fact it was she who had thought of bringing champagne. Bob Moran was preoccupied with stomach pains and wondered if he was getting an ulcer. George was frantic from Malfoof's driving and Barbie was numbed by the thought of Doris and George being together again. And so, to the casual observer, it was a somber group that approached Reginald's door. They stood, faces composed, waiting for him to answer their knock.

None of them even noticed the fat little girl in pink slacks as she pushed through the shrubbery to the back of the house. She knocked three times on the cellar door before Francis, her smiling host, let her in.

Upstairs, Reginald, trying to smile, opened the door to his guests and said "Come in, come in" as he thought, I wish I were dead.

"Oh Sacred Heart of Jesus, I put my trust in Thee." Hans stood at his attic window praying for deliverance. "St. Joseph, protect me."

He watched the fat little girl push through the shrubbery and run to the cellar entry into which, after a minute, she disappeared. Somebody in their club, he thought, and his mind went back to his own youth when chastity had never been a problem.

"I give You my heart and my soul," he said, and went to take another icy shower.

They were making desultory conversation about Kent State, repeating yet again the improbabilities, the cruelties, the mad abuse of power in this country. Doris kept her rhetoric in control, however, and George had not yet recovered from Doris' cruel refusal, and so the burden of enthusiasm fell upon Bob Moran. He had been vaguely distraught ever since the raid on the draft board—his cheek was twitching all the time now—and tonight his enthusiasm for causes, good or bad, was slight. Reginald found himself wondering what any of them—Natalie excepted—was doing here.

Though none of them—Natalie excepted—knew it, what they were doing was making a ritual pilgrimage to the shrine of Reginald. Their motives, like the motives of all pilgrims, were complex, an entanglement of hope and disbelief and a conviction that somewhere at the center of their pilgrimage love was to be found. Theirs, moreover, was a modern pilgrimage and thus intended, at least in part, to demonstrate to their saint that while they admired him they did not need him, that what must be done they had done on their own, without his help or interference, that they forgave him his inefficacy and rather liked him anyhow. It was not actually triumphalism. Natalie, who had been reading the *Summa Theologica*, knew what it was: a kind of self-satisfaction which, like St. Thomas' "good," tends by its nature to diffuse itself.

The conversation, desultory to begin with, soon wound down to discussion of the weather. Doris could stand it no longer.

"We've got something to tell you, Reg. Natalie too, of course." She looked at Natalie, that beautiful hard face concealing God knows what, and she swallowed and went on. "You know how we talked the other night about the draft board? Well, we did it."

Everyone sat straight and leaned forward a little, waiting for Reginald's response as if it were some kind of benediction.

"No kidnapping," she added, "no bombing."

"You're joking," Reginald said.

"Dead serious. Even in the Koran it says . . ."

"Why don't I make us all a drink," he said, and everyone agreed eagerly, so eagerly that Doris' misquotation of Mohammed was lost to everyone except Malfoof who forgave her because she was a desert rose and a sweet well of passion.

"Come on," Francis said, "do it my way."

"No," she said, "I don't like it that way."

"Why not? That's how they all do it nowadays. Everybody does. It's in books and everything."

"No, I won't. It's a sin that way."

"Come on," he said. "Lookit."

Michael poked his head from behind the trunk and looked at his brother with envy and hatred.

"No," she said, "it tastes like turnips and I hate turnips."

"Okay for you. If you don't do it my way, I won't fuck you any more."

"See if I care."

They stood facing one another. Judy thought of making a bargain—she would do it if he would kiss her—and then another thought came to her, that she didn't have to do anything she didn't want.

"You better care. I'll spread the word on you. Your mother will find out."

"I'll tell your father about the molotov cocktails and the dynamite. I'll tell the police."

"Get out of here, you pig."

"It will be a pleasure," she said in her mother's tones as she crossed to the cellar door.

"Fat fuck, fat shitty ass," he shouted.

Judy turned at the door intending to return the insult, but Francis was coming toward her with the stick of dynamite in his hand and, terrified, she slammed the cellar door and ran across the back yard.

From the attic Hans saw her try to climb the fence, give up, and then disappear around the front of the house. He paid no attention, preoccupied as he was with eternal damnation.

In the cellar Francis turned on Michael, but he refused to play Judy's part. Thinking it better not to force the issue–Michael was crazy these days and might tell anything–Francis challenged him to the shot put, as he called it. Side by side they masturbated to see who could shoot farther. Francis, as always, was the winner by several feet.

After the first drink Doris and Malfoof got the champagne from the car and, in no time, the pilgrimage had turned into a celebration. Kent State was forgotten in the excited reliving of their own act of civil disobedience.

"George was the one," Barbie was explaining. "You

should have seen George. He took right over and was he ever something! He broke down the door and we just tore right in."

"No, that was the whole thing. I *didn't* break down the door. That was the irony of the situation. I kept thinking to myself that I didn't want to break the lock and all of a sudden it came to me, here I am about to break into the draft board and destroy records and risk life imprisonment, and I'm worried about a lock. A lock!"

Everyone laughed, enjoying the irony, except Natalie and Reginald who merely looked at one another.

"The best part, though," Doris said, "was *how* we got the lock open. You know how they use a strip of celluloid to break into hotel rooms? Well, we did too. You'll never guess what. With a Roman collar we found in the Jesuit car!"

Bob Moran smiled through his twitch. He was not sure he liked reliving the scene this way.

Barbie took up the story. "I mean it was perfect because George is still a priest, officially anyway"—here she closed her hand over his—"and I'm still a nun, and we use a Roman collar to break in. I mean, what could be more beautiful?"

"I mean, wow!" Doris said.

"I am doing this for my Doris, my little ayni, and because I spit on Panthers."

"The thing is, everyone was really terrif," Doris said. "We were a team, a real revolutionary unit with one shared intention and one shared result, and we did it."

Everyone nodded solemnly, for it was true; they *had* been terrif.

They opened another bottle of champagne.

Hans heard the champagne cork and smiled bitterly to himself. Heathens, he thought, fiddling while Rome burns. May God forgive them.

He considered going down to the second floor to talk to Billy, but Billy was doing a research paper on Sheldon's theory of personality and all he had talked about for the past two weeks was endomorphs and ectomorphs, and Hans was sick of being cited as the classic example of the endomorph.

He leafed through an old Spiritual Light Book, saved from the novitiate. "Oh, be swift to love! Make haste to be kind." "A glad heart maketh a cheerful countenance." "Joy, joy at the end!" It went on and on like that; Hans was not interested.

He stuck his thumb in between the pages very near the end of the book and found himself in the juniorate section. "Look thy last on all things lovely every hour." Walter de la Mare. He shook his head; he could not remember who Walter de la Mare was, some nut like Sean probably.

Discouraged, he flipped to the final page of the notebook. Printed there in purple and green ink, the lettering as Gothic as he had been able to make it, he found "Ecclesiastes."

To everything there is a season.
    And a time to every purpose under the heaven:
A time to be born and a time to die;
    A time to plant and a time to pluck that
      which is planted;
A time to kill, and a time to heal;

He put the notebook down. He was going to do it again, he knew he was. Not the prayers, the exercises, the memory work, the showers, not any of it had worked. Once again he would masturbate and once again, until he could get to confession, he would be damned forever.

"Oh God," he said, "you've *got* to help me. You promised!"

And at once the thought came to him, "Rise and take Mary and the Child and go into the land of Egypt."

All very well for Joseph, but how on earth could he get out of the house with all those maniacs drinking and yelling downstairs? "I will be a pillar of cloud before you and a pillar of fire by night."

Excited, relieved, he began to take off his clothes. He would shower, a ritual purification like the Israelites before the Exodus, and then he would put on his black suit and his Roman collar, and he would go and tell old Father Sheehey everything. God would deliver him yet.

"Here's a good one we can make. Napalm. All you need is two-parts gasoline to one-part soap flakes."

"It won't work."

"It will too."

"What good is it?"

"It's what the Americans drop on the jungle in Vietnam and it all burns up."

"Niggers don't live in jungles. Not in Roxbury."

"Go get the soapsuds, and shut up."

Michael returned from the McReedy side of the cellar with a bar of Ivory soap.

"Stupid shit. Flakes! Get the Rinso or whatever's there. You can't use a bar of soap."

"You're so smart, why don't you do it yourself." But he got Francis the soapflakes anyway.

Michael was bored with pretending they would attack the Panthers. He was bored with molotov cocktails he would never get to throw. He was bored with Fucky, a smartass bully, and he was fed up with being treated like a shit.

"Pour a cupful of gas into that soup dish," Francis said. He himself was busy measuring out a half-cup of laundry detergent. "And put that can on the floor where you won't knock it over."

Michael measured out the cup of gasoline and placed the can off to the side where it would be out of the way. He watched while Francis mixed the soapflakes and the gasoline. It certainly didn't look like much.

"It's never gonna work."

"It'll work. Go get me one of Ma's coffee jars.

Michael started up the stairs.

"An empty one, Mucky."

"So the next thing is, we're all going to fly to D.C. and turn ourselves in at the rally on the ninth."

Reginald said nothing.

"Well, what do you think?"

"It's your funeral," Reginald said and toasted them with the last of the champagne.

"Our funeral," they said together and raised their glasses to the toast. Who needed Reginald, anyhow.

At that moment Hans, incongruously clerical in his black suit, stepped through the doorway and said to the raised glasses, "Excuse me, please, I have an appointment to keep." He went through the kitchen and out the back door.

Michael had brought back a full jar of Maxwell House coffee and provoked Francis further by lighting a cigarette in front of him. Francis punched him in the face, harder than usual, and Michael stumbled backward into the can of gasoline. It tipped over, the yellow liquid gushing out in a thick stream that ran zigzag across the cellar floor.

"God damn you. Now look what you've done." Francis punched his brother in the stomach.

"All right, Fucky, you asked for it," Michael said.

Slowly, deliberately, with Francis watching him, he struck a match and dropped it into the little stream at his feet. Instantly flames shot halfway to the ceiling, a sheet of fire stood between them.

"Fucky, I didn't mean it, Fucky," Michael screamed.

Michael had expected the fire to flare up and immediately burn itself out, but the flames flickered and crackled along the zigzag path of gasoline. "Help," he began to shout. "Help me!"

"Come on, you shit," Francis said.

Reaching through the flames, he grabbed his brother's arm and pulled him toward the entrance to the McReedy part of the cellar. Wildly they scrambled up the stairs and out the door.

In the back yard Hans was taking deep breaths after his ordeal with that crowd in the living room. "My Help and my Deliverer," he said, smiling up at the stars.

The McReedys crashed into him and Michael, in tears, fell full length on the ground. Francis yanked him up and shouting, "For Chrissake, let's get out of here," he vaulted the back fence with Michael close behind.

Hans walked to the cellar entrance and looked down the stairs. He could see a light flickering somewhere on the Thomasite side of the house. He considered for a moment whether it would be better to turn off the light or continue on his spiritual errand. Turning off the light would take only a minute and it would be an act of the virtue of poverty. Yes, pick up a pin, as the Little Flower said, and save a soul.

Hans descended the cellar stairs slowly—he had never been down there before—pausing on the last step to tug his suit jacket straight in front and to check his collar for neatness and comfort. Entering the Thomasite part of the cellar, he squared his shoulders and cleared his throat as if he were on his way to an interview with a dignitary.

He was alarmed to see that the light was in fact a tiny fire. The gasoline had quickly burned itself out and all that remained was a little puddle over in the corner. "Those darned kids," he said aloud, "they could have caused a fire."

He looked around for something to smother the flames with. He thought of stamping them out, it would have been easy to do, but he was wearing his good shoes and he didn't want to stain them. And then he spotted the pile of rags. He removed his jacket and placed it neatly on one of the trunks. And then he took an armful of the rags and placed them firmly on the flames.

That should do it, he thought, and that thought was his last.

There was an explosion and, at once, a whole series of explosions as the molotov cocktails he had knocked to the floor went off like miniature cannon shot. The huge explosion that followed was made by the stick of dynamite as it tore through Hans' bent shoulders, decapitating him and spattering the cellar walls with bits of his limbs and clotted sections of his insides.

It was only because the larger part of his head remained intact that investigators later were able to establish that the body was, in fact, that of Hans Berger, O.S.T. Despite the condition of the cellar these same investigators learned a great deal more; they were Catholic, however, and suppressed for the sake of the Church at large the incontrovertible evidence that the cellar had been not only a revolutionary hangout but the site of sex orgies as well.

As Hans placed the rags and the dynamite firmly on

the flames, thinking, that should do it, Natalie in the room above had just said it was time for her to go. Everyone said yes, it was time to go, and they all stood, satisfied and a little dizzy.

A series of explosions sent them all to the windows. And then suddenly a huge blast tore a hole in the floor of Reginald's bedroom. In the living room, pictures fell off the walls and chairs hopped about and turned over. Barbie began to scream as she and George bolted for the back door. The house trembled and then lurched crazily to one side. As flames shot through the floor of Reginald's bedroom, Doris and Malfoof, Natalie and Reginald and Bob Moran edged through the kitchen and out the tilted door into the safety of the back yard.

The rest of the night was a series of confusions, a dim nightmare they all remembered differently, but which they always thought of first whenever they thought of the spring of 1970.

Firemen appeared out of nowhere and swung with fervor into their work of chopping chairs and breaking crockery, destroying anything fragile or flammable before the fire could get to it. Policemen surrounded the house and kept the crowd at a safe distance. Only the photographers had free run of the place. It was one of them who put a ladder up to the second floor and saved Billy Biggins who had heard all the noise outside and wondered what was going on. No one found Hans, or what remained of him, until the next afternoon when investigators began poking through the rubble.

Through the beautiful spring night the house burned on and on until, just before dawn, it crumpled into itself, leaving only a black and smoldering staircase that rose to a vanished second floor. The staircase appeared in all the newspapers the next day, eerie against the morning sky, and with it were other pictures—of the house burning, of Bob Moran vomiting into the bushes, and a great many of Doris Hanlon, the fuel heiress, in her silver harem dress.

Doris' costume had been the principal attraction of the evening, first of all at the fire, and then later when she and Malfoof carried Bob Moran into Holy Ghost hospital, and later still when she joined the others for coffee at Bickfords. With the night over and the house gone, none of them had anything further to say to one another, they discovered, and so they drank their coffee in silence, glancing hazily at the newspapers, and then they went home.

Doris and Malfoof went back to Doris' apartment. George and Barbie, not to be outdone, went back to Barbie's. Natalie went alone to her own apartment where she knelt down, as was her custom, and meditated for an hour on Christ's injunctions to the Pharisees.

Reginald had no place to go, so he phoned Father Sheehey who smiled and nodded and said of course he must come over at once, that Billy and Jim had moved in already. And so Reginald returned to the old house on Winter Place where there was no protest and not much poverty and obedience. But everyone there was holy, or at least meant to be.